AMRITSAR
A Year in a Timeless City

CA Davinder Singh
Nihal Parashar

© CA Davinder Singh **2019**

All rights reserved

All rights reserved by author. No part of this publication may be reproduced, stored in a retrieval system or transmitted in any form or by any means, electronic, mechanical, photocopying, recording or otherwise, without the prior permission of the author.

Although every precaution has been taken to verify the accuracy of the information contained herein, the author and publisher assume no responsibility for any errors or omissions. No liability is assumed for damages that may result from the use of information contained within.

First Published in November 2019

ISBN: 978-93-5347-902-2

BLUE ROSE PUBLISHERS
www.bluerosepublishers.com
info@bluerosepublishers.com
+91 8882 898 898

Written by:
CA Davinder Singh & Nihal Parashar

Editor:
Shubha Guru

Illustrations:
Jaspal Singh

Design:
Rohit Kumar Rai

Cover Photographs:
Nihal Parashar

Distributed by: Blue Rose, Amazon, Flipkart, Shopclues

Contents

Foreword by CA Davinder Singh	06
Foreword by Nihal Parashar	10
Introduction	13
Amritsar City Chronology	15
Maps of Amritsar	21

Part 1: A year in a timeless city

January	26
February	31
March	36
April	41
May	45
June	50
July	55
August	60
September	65
October	71
November	76
December	81

Part 2: History written on the walls

The City That Is Amritsar	88
The Bloody Massacre In Amritsar	95
Partition Of India	103
Nineteen Sixty Five	111
Nineteen Eighty Four	117
Wagah Border and Diplomacy	125

Part 3: Amritsari

Sudarshan Kapoor	134
Surinder Kochar	136
Vinay Mehra	138
RJ Heer	140
Sudhir Mehra	142
Chandan Prabhakar	144
Arun Kapoor	146
Mina Chugh	148
Bobby Badshah	150
Joginder Singh	152
Rajinder and Gunvant Sachdeva	154
Surinder Singh	156
Acknowledgement	159
Reference	161
About the authors	162

Foreword
by CA Davinder Singh

My bond with the city of Amritsar is more than 150 years old. While most people have settled here after the 1947 partition, I am a sixth generation Amritsari. Before the partition, Amritsar was a Muslim dominated city. In fact, Lahore and Amritsar were tagged as twin cities, having the same culture, language and traditions. Amritsar is only 450 years old, founded by fourth Sikh Guru Shri Guru Ram Dass Ji. It is known as the epicentre of Sikhism and home to what we call, mecca of Sikhs, the Golden Temple. Amritsar (amrit sarovar) is named after its sweet drinking water which translates as the pool of nectar.

The history of the city dates back 200 years. Maharaja Ranjit Singh, the Sikh ruler, brought trade and prosperity to the city in the year 1802. All major trades of the city like tea, shawls, dry fruits have flourished during the reign of Maharaja.

Amritsar is both traditional and modern in terms of culture. People are mostly soft spoken, hospitable, humble and easy going. Their sense of fashion is amazing. It is usually said that fashion directly comes to Amritsar after Mumbai. I fondly call my city Amritsar a resort city where people prefer to live in houses rather than apartments. An ordinary Amritsari lives leisurely at his own pace with decent earning and less expenditure. Businesses usually do good here, thanks to the thousands of daily visitors to the Golden Temple.

The purpose to pen down this piece of work in the shape of a book is to share the story of my city to my own fellow Amritsaris and especially with my children. The sole purpose of writing this book is to document the vibrant lifestyle of the city. There are countless interesting stories about Amritsari lifestyle, our knack for food and of course the warm hospitality for what we are known for. These are worth sharing with the world.

The book is divided into three parts where the first part of the book is about the lifestyle of Amritsaris. The whole city life is explained in these chapters of twelve months in the interest of readers. The idea to divide city life in twelve months is inspired by the 'Barah Maha', a chapter in Gurbani from our sacred scripture Sri Guru Granth Sahib Ji. It describes the importance of every month in our daily lives. The first day of every month is observed as Sangrand and the verses from Barah Maha of that particular month is recited at our homes and all the Gurudwaras across the world since ages. In the holy Golden Temple, the Gurbani is sung in different Ragas relevant to every month and time of the day. In the book, the Punjabi months go side by side English calendar months. In the beginning of every chapter of the month, verses from Barah Maha of that particular month are briefly described to let readers understand the importance of the month. Every month has its own significance in day to day life of Amritsaris.

Since Amritsar experiences all the six seasons in a year unlike many other parts of the world, the lifestyle also changes after every two months. Amritsaris have something new to experience in terms of festivals, food, flora and fauna, every month. Temperatures vary a lot; weather is extremely cold in December and it gets very hot in June. The post winter rainfall in the month of April and pre-winter rainfall in October add more charm to the beauty of the city. The style of living, clothing and the way people consume food here changes every month.

The second part narrates the major historical events of the city in the last 100 years. The section 'History written on the wall' shows our indomitable spirit of fighting with every adversity and bouncing back. Amritsar has witnessed four major historical tragedies during the last 100 years. We have experienced these unfortunate events once every three decades in the last century. From Jallianwala Bagh massacre in 1919 to Partition riots in 1947 and Indo Pak War in 1965. The latest in history is the year 1984, Operation Blue Star, a military operation inside Golden Temple. Despite all these tragedies, Amritsar has always emerged more vibrant than before with the blessings of Shri Guru Ram Dass Ji.

The third part of the book is about the life experiences of people of Amritsar in the section 'Amritsari'. It may be of interest to the readers that some old residents of Amritsar have shared their memories about Lahore and Amritsar. These interesting nuggets add flavour to the book. Readers will get to know about the life experiences of people during 1947 partition, 1965 Indo Pak war and 1984 Operation Blue star.

During this journey of one year of writing this book, my own understanding of the city and its glorious history has multiplied manifold. The respect for the city with a sense of pride is the key result of this project, which shall give a sense of gratitude to the readers. I happen to meet so many wonderful people during this journey of writing, who are much wiser than me and have helped me in completing this project.

My sincere thanks to Surinder Kochar, a dear friend and a highly respected historian of the city for spending many days with us during this project. I am thankful to Sudarshan Kapoor for encouraging me to write about city life.

I humbly dedicate this piece of work to my father Rajinder Singh Sachdeva and mother Gunwant, a beautiful couple, who supported me in every possible manner.

I am thankful to my beloved wife Dolly, daughters Avneet and Anurit and my son-in-law Jasraj who tolerated my persistent absence from their lives during this project.

I am delighted to have worked along with the very talented Nihal Parashar. This project would not have seen the light of the day without his brilliant writing.

I am grateful to Jaspal, a young artist from the city, who did his work brilliantly. His illustrations have brought this book to life.

I am thankful to all the various authors and producers of original works along with all the people who helped me in writing this book. A separate acknowledgements section at the end of the narrative lists these in detail.

I consider this book of mine as a gift to the amazing people of Amritsar whether they are living in the city or outside.

I have seen my city moving at the same pace since childhood. Not much has changed in our life including the cat naps post-lunch. One of the distinguishing features of the city is that people here earn like those in the metropolitan cities, but their expenditures are much less than them. The younger generation prefers to settle abroad these days. Perhaps this attempt of mine will make them understand that today Amritsar is a window to the world with huge potential and one can make a good fortune by living here.

Amritsar
August 25, 2019.   **CA Davinder Singh**

Foreword
by Nihal Parashar

Amritsar has always fascinated me. The fact that Amritsar and Lahore were earlier twin cities made me realise that the city has many stories that needed to be unfolded. When we think about Lahore it seems like a faraway place. However, it isn't that far, we are divided by a border and collective hatred.

While I was studying at Delhi, I and my friends made several plans to visit Amritsar but sadly it never materialised. It was after moving to Mumbai many years later, I got a chance to meet Davinder who shared his idea about writing a book on Amritsar. The idea was intriguing and the chance to get to know the city was something I could never let go off my hands. Davinder gave insights about the city's history and day to day life while I explored the city like an outsider who luckily got to spend a lot of time in the city.

In the process of writing this book, I stayed in Amritsar for a good amount of time. Talking to Davinder gave me an idea of the city and what Amritsar is all about. I got a chance to talk to numerous people. Also, there were moments when I would just roam around in the walled city of Amritsar and just observe people.

I am not sure if I have been able to write all of it in the book. As a matter of fact, I have not been able to write it at all. It is difficult to write a conversation with an old hakim about the changes he has seen over the last five decades or so. He has seen a change which cannot be captured in words. It is difficult to frame everything in sentences. And while writing the book, I pondered over the thought if we can ever capture all our thoughts and conversations into words. And do we really need to capture it? Can't simpler words do justice to what a city stands for? These are the complex questions about which I happened to think about a lot while working on this book.

Davinder and I had a clarity that we are not writing an academic book on Amritsar. It is a book of memories. The book is mainly divided into three parts, months in the city, the people of the city and historical events in the city.

Davinder really surprised me with his love for Amritsar. His pure love for the city gave me a perspective to see it with different eyes and I won't hesitate to say that I fell for this city. Over the last one year, I visited the city a lot and I am sure I will still be coming back here even after finishing this book.

Haven't you ever had the feeling that cities give out energies and have the power to accept or reject you just like people? Amritsar has accepted me, and I am glad that it did. Some cities have the power to transform you as a person and this city did the same for me. Amritsar is really a divine city, it accepts everyone.

The city is home to the holy Golden Temple. Every conversation about Amritsar is incomplete without mentioning the Golden Temple. The temple is mesmerizing. I have spent hours in the temple complex, doing nothing. There is something about the Golden Temple that is difficult to write. It must be experienced.

More than anything else, I am thankful that this book happened to me. Please note that it is our understanding of the city and not absolute truth. This is what Davinder and I could write on Amritsar. Of course, there is much left unsaid, much left unwritten.

I am thankful to the people who gave me a chance to talk to

them and share their idea about this city while writing this book, especially Surinder Kochar and Sudarshan Kapoor Ji. Their insights were really helpful. I am thankful to Vinay Mehra, who is a true Amritsari friend I was looking for. I have such fond memories of roaming around Amritsar with Vinay. I am thankful to Dolly Sachdeva for probably the best food Amritsar could offer me.

I am thankful to Jaspal for the most wonderful illustrations of the city. I am glad that my friend Shubha agreed to help as an editor for our book. I always knew she was the one whom I would approach for any editing related work. I am also thankful to Rohit for helping in designing the book. Working with Rohit was a wonderful experience which I will always cherish.

Lastly, I am thankful to Sweety, my wife, who supported me with her understanding of historical perspective of the city. The historical section of the book could not have been completed if she was not there. Her support was vital in completing the book.

The book is in your hands. The city will change. People will change. The new generation will take over. We are glad that we could capture a moment from the timeless city in the form of this book.

Happy reading.

Mumbai
August 27, 2019. **Nihal Parashar**

Introduction

There is no easy answer to the question, what is Amritsar? What we can do is share our understanding of the city, our memories and our version of stories about Amritsar. To understand a beautiful and complex city like Amritsar, one needs to devote many hours and years of his/her life.

If you ask a native, he'll say "you'll not realise the importance of Amritsar in your life unless you move away". It is true isn't it? We don't miss things when they are right in front of us, we mostly take it for granted, except when are away and we miss it.

The people of Amritsar have invested decades in developing the food culture of the city. Any Amritsari can talk for hours about the food of Amritsar. Especially about its magical water which is considered to be the reason for tasty food in Amritsar. However, it is true that sometimes the food in Amritsar can be rich in calories. The 'round belly' of an average Amritsari is evidently visible, but still people do not quit eating street food. The taste of the street food is unforgettable, however, if you keep eating it, you shall turn obese. So, decide wisely.

There is no doubt about the fact that the people of Amritsar are sweet. They genuinely believe that they must serve the visitors of Amritsar as it is one way to serve Guru Ramdass Ji, the founder of the city. An average Amritsari interacts with people of myriad nationalities in their lifetime as Amritsar is one of the most visited cities in India. This gives global exposure to the people of Amritsar right at home. People meet many guests and are always ready to be the perfect host. Amritsaris truly want everybody to spread positivity about city.

The water of Amritsar is nectar for its people. What else can explain the positive attitude of a city which has been attacked brutally every few decades? What keeps the city going? It can't be explained in words but if you ask any Amritsari, most of them will say, by the blessing of the Gurus.

Amritsar is a survivor. It survived the invaders from the west during Maharaja Ranjit Singh's era. It survived the bloody massacre in 1919 and witnessed the greatest Indian tragedy of 1947. Amritsar was at a critical juncture at that time. It saw the 1965 war between India and Pakistan and survived. The city witnessed another dark phase in the year 1984 and braved that too.

Arguably, Amritsar is a very new city. While there are cities in India which have a history of a couple of millennia, Amritsar has a history of only five centuries. We cannot ignore the fact that in these many years, it has become one of the most important cities on the planet, fondly called the Vatican of Sikhism by many across the globe.

This book tries to give you an idea about living in Amritsar and provide an insight into the lives of the locals. We don't claim it to be accurate and true for everyone. Different people may have different versions of the same story, same place. Our idea is to know more about the beautiful city of Amritsar. The city deserves a thousand books, and even then, we all would not know what made the city so special.

Amritsar City Chronology

1574: The land was bought by Guru Ram Dass Ji, which later became Ram Dass Pur

1577: Construction of the Sarovar by Guru Ram Dass Ji started

1589: Shri Guru Arjan Dev Ji, the Fifth Sikh Guru, completed the construction work of the Sarovar and laid the foundation stone through Hazrat Miyaan Mir

1601: Construction of Shri Harmandir Sahib, the Golden Temple, completed

1604: Shri Guru Granth Sahib, the Holy book, was compiled and completed at Gurudwara Ramsar, which is approximately 200 meters away from the Golden Temple

1604: Shri Guru Granth Sahib was placed inside the Golden Temple and Baba Budda Ji was appointed the first head priest

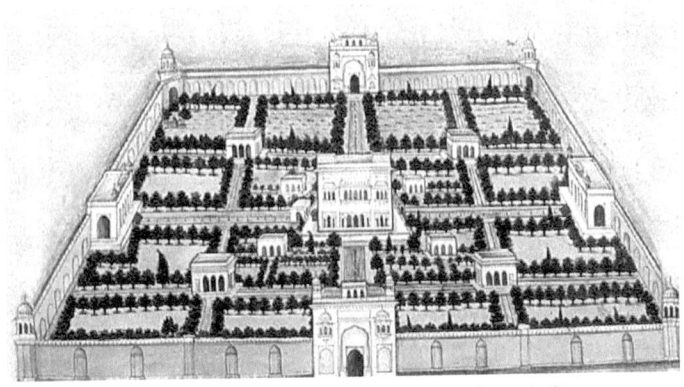

Archival painting of the Rambagh Garden; Source: British Library Archives

1607: Shri Guru Hargobind Sahib laid the foundation stone of Akal Takht

1621: Shri Guru Teg Bahadur, the Ninth Sikh Guru, was born in Gurudwara Guru Ka Mahal, near Guru Bazaar, which is approximately 100 meters away from the Golden Temple

1621: The first battle between Shri Guru Hargobind Ji and the Mughals took place

1621: Shri Guru Hargobind Ji shifted from Amritsar and created a new city named Keeratpur, near Anandpur Sahib, in Ropar.

1664: Shri Guru Teg Bahadur Ji, the Ninth Sikh Guru, returned to Amritsar to visit the Golden Temple

1721: Bhai Mani Singh was appointed the head priest of the Golden Temple

1738-39: The royal army of Nadir Shah forcefully occupied the Golden Temple. During Diwali, the Royal Army stopped Sikhs from entering the Golden Temple and arrested Bhai Mani Singh. Bhai Mani Singh was later martyred in Lahore.

1740: The Golden Temple was re-occupied by the Sikhs

1748: Sardar Jassa Singh Ahluwalia killed Nazim Salabat Khan

1756-57: Taimur, son of Ahmad Shah Abdali, demolished the Golden Temple

1757: Baba Deep Singh Ji fought to free the Golden Temple and was martyred

1762: Ahmad Shah Abdali destroyed Harmandir Sahib again,

19th Century image of Gobindgarh Fort

and filled the holy Sarovar with sand

1764: Work for the reconstruction of Harmandir Sahib started

1802: Maharaja Ranjit Singh's reign begins in Amritsar

1806-09: Qila Gobindgarh was constructed

1822-24: The city of Amritsar was fortified, and 12 gates were created by the order of Maharaja Ranjit Singh

1849: Amritsar became a district under the British rule

1858: Amritsar was connected by rail to Lahore and Multan

1867: The first magazine of the Golden Temple was published

1870: Amritsar was connected by rail to Delhi

1871: The Kuka agitation started

1872: Bhai Vir Singh was born

1874: Guru Singh Sabha was established

1885: Masjid Khisruddin was constructed

1892: Foundation stone of Khalsa College was laid down

1902: Foundation stone of Gurudwara Saragarhi was laid down

1904: Central Khalsa orphanage was established

1919: Jallianwala Bagh massacre took place

1919: Annual conference of Indian National Congress (INC) was held in Amritsar

1920: Shiromani Gurudwara Prabandhak Committee (SGPC) was established

Fortifications, gateways and moat at the Gobindgarh Fort

1920: Agitation of Keys (Chhabiyon ka Morcha) took place, which is considered ignition of the freedom movement. Mahatma Gandhi congratulated over the victory

1921: Durgayana Temple was established

1922: Agitation of Guru Ka Bagh was started

1923: Kar Seva of Golden Temple Sarovar completed

1924: Jaito agitation started

1926: Punjabi Sabha started

1931: Sarai Guru Ram Dass foundation stone was laid

1947: Partition of India took place. Amritsar witnessed major riots and mass migration

1954: Bhagat Pooran Singh established Pingalwada

1956: Central Sikh Museum was established

1960: Sant Fatah Singh started an agitation for Punjabi Sooba

1961: Master Tara Singh joined the Punjabi Sooba movement

1965: Indo-Pak war took place. Amritsar witnessed the horrors of war

1969: Guru Nanak Dev University was established

1973: Kar Seva of Sarovar completed

1975: Agitation by Akalis against emergency.

1977: Guru Ram Dass Hospital was established

1984: Operation Blue Star took place

1986: Corridor around Golden Temple was built, and many shops were relocated

2016: Partition museum was established

2016: Heritage street around the Golden temple was created

Maps of Amritsar

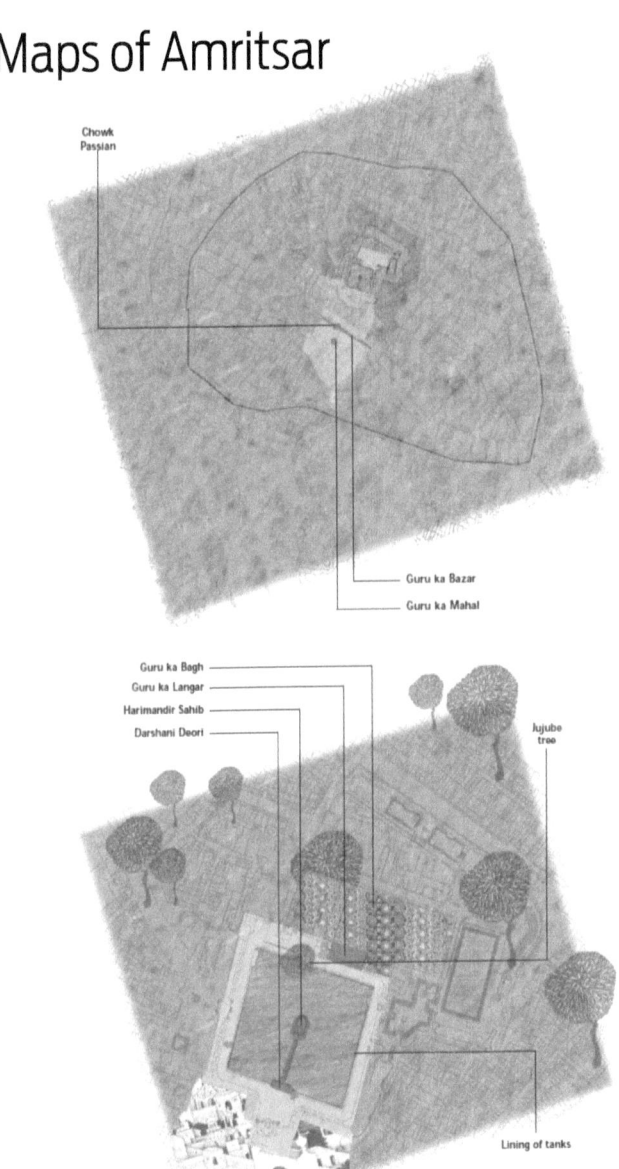

Amritsar: Changes made between 1573 AD and 1606 AD

Amritsar walled City in 1870

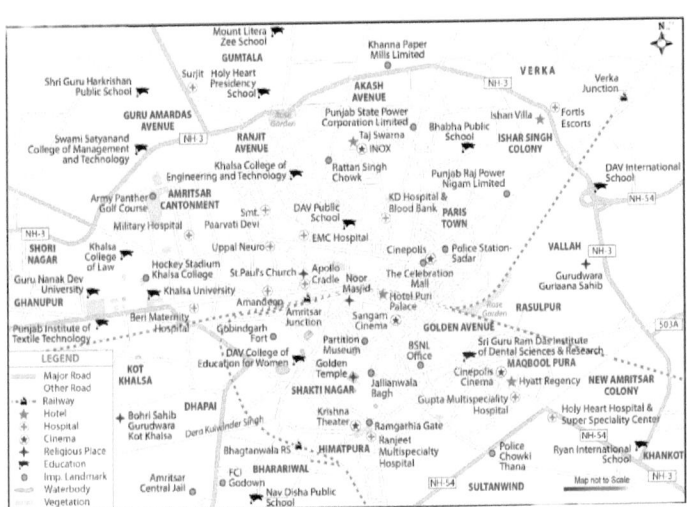

Present Map of Amritsar

Part 1
A Year in a Timeless City

JANUARY
Poh-Magh

Mâgh(i) majjan sung(i) sâdhuâ(n) dhûrhî kar(i) isnân(u)
Her(i) kâ nâm(u) dhiâey sun(i) sabhnâ no kar(i) dân(u)

(In the month of Mâgh people go to holy places and consider it a pious deed. But he who recognises the pilgrimage in his heart, his life is sanctified.)

We've entered the month of January; the enthusiasm of people in Amritsar is at its festive best. People are hosting get-togethers, partying and planning getaways to celebrate the new year. There isn't any dearth of places to celebrate in this holy city; everyone has a place to go irrespective of their social class. After all, everyone is looking forward to have a good time and the city doesn't disappoint.

The month of January also marks the beginning of the month of Magh, it starts from Jan 14. It's the 11th month as per the Hindu calendar, celebrations continue throughout the month of January in Amritsar. Adding to the celebrations is amazing food available here and during winter months. Gur ka Halwa and Maide ki Khajoor are certainly not to be missed.

A typical January day

January is known to be extremely cold in Amritsar. There is a period of almost 15 days when the city does not see the sun. We do know that the sun is out there somewhere but the thick fog makes it difficult to see anything. If you talk about city's geography, it is not very far from the great Himalayas. Thus the gift of fog, if we can call it, is bestowed upon the city. The temperature in January can go as low as 1 degree Celsius. Record shows that the lowest recorded temperature in January is -3.5 degree Celsius!

Generally, people are very fond of whiskey in Amritsar. However, they move over to Rum (with hot water) to beat the cold during harsh winters. There are some very popular bars in the city that are thronged by natives for evening drinks. Some of the popular ones include Amritsar Club, Service Club and Lumsden Club (accessible only to members and their guests). Most famous ones are British era clubs located inside the beautiful Ram Bagh Gardens. It once used to be the summer palace of the only Sikh king Ranjit Singh.

Throughout the day, people can be seen warming themselves along the roadside by burning woods. It is where you listen to the best commentary on national politics.

Lohri celebration

Lohri is a popular folk festival in Punjab. The thirteenth day of January is celebrated as the day of Lohri. People believe that the festival commemorates the passing of the winter solstice and since ages, it also celebrated as winter crop season. Lohri is observed a night before Makar Sankranti, which is also known as Maghi. The day of Lohri in Amritsar is a visual treat as the sky is filled with kites, people play music on rooftops, and get busy in celebrations. Old Amritsar, or the walled city as people call it, also witnesses unofficial kite competitions. Next day, on Makar Sankranti people mostly

indulge in charity besides visiting various holy places. It is customary for every family member to offer handful of rice and money to the poor.

Food thoughts in January
No blinking at the fact that January is the month for great food (but which month is not!). Here are some recommendations if you wish to visit Amritsar during January:

Novelty Sweets at Lawrence Road is where one can get the best Gur Ka Halwa and evening snacks. For years, it has been a go-to place for the people of Amritsar for some amazing sweets. Novelty Sweets has been part of the people's memory for decades now. In fact, the square where the shop is located is known as Novelty Chowk. Another popular junction for food is Lawrence Road. If you wish to try Amritsar's version of fruit cream, do remember Sukhram. It serves one of

Amritsar's very specific versions of ice creams. Kanha sweets and Kanhaya Sweets, on the other hand, are very popular with the tourists for Poori. You can also head to Mathura Chat for evening snacks.

Food scenes in Amritsar are incomplete without talking about scrumptious fish delicacies. Amritsari fish is being served all across the country but the real taste is unique to this city. Out of the three most famous varieties of fishes, Sole, Singara and Basa, the first one is the most expensive. Singara is commonly used in delicacies and Basa is generally not preferred. The most talked about Sole fish dishes are available at Lumsden club, which sadly has a limited entrance. Others famous joints include Crystal Restaurant located at the chowk with the same name and Astoria, in Ranjit Avenue.

The biggest fish market of the city is Hall Bazaar. A typical morning in this bazaar is filled with customers bargaining with shopkeepers and buying their favourite fishes.

FEBRUARY
Magh-Phagun

Phalgun(i) anand upârjanâHer(i) sajjan pargatey âey
Sant sahâî Râm ke kar(i) kirpâ dîâ milâey

(After the severe months of winter comes the colour riot month of Phagun. Those who have the presence of the Lord in their hearts enjoy spiritual bliss.)

The beautiful part of the Shabad Kirtan (hymns from the Holy book Guru Granth Sahib) sung at Golden Temple is that they resonate with the ongoing season. February is the season of Basant, the Shabad Kirtan in Basant Raga can be heard at the Golden Temple throughout the Phagun month (starts mid-February). These kirtans are very soothing to ears and quite easy to understand if you are familiar with Hindi and Punjabi languages. One can spend hours listening to these kirtans in the Golden Temple.

Unlike January, winter in February isn't extensively cold but don't get very comfortable. It can surprise you when you are least expecting it.

February is the season of Magh and Phagun. Phagun is the last month of the Indian lunar calendar. Many writers have written poems and verses describing the beauty of Phagun. It is the arrival of the spring season. Traditionally it is believed that winters will end in Phagun. But not now. The seasons must have shifted in all these years. Just after Magh (mid-February), Sun would change its path, and slowly warmth in the season would fade in.

This is the season of weddings – the fat Punjabi Indian weddings take place in Amritsar. Among Sikhs, there is no culture of matching Janam Patri or Tewa (matching horoscopes of bride and groom). People do not look for any specific muhurat or auspicious day for marriages. A convenient date and day is chosen - which is generally a Sunday, keeping in mind the exams of children in the family! As a matter of fact, dates of marriages are chosen like this throughout the year. The only exceptions for marriages are a 10-day period of Holi in March and a 15-day period of Shraddh, generally in August. Apart from these all days are equal for Amritsari Sikhs. All you need is the availability of marriage hall in Amritsar.

The visible change in weather
There has been a dramatic change of weather in Amritsar's February. Two decades back February was not as cold as it is now. Now February feels like an extension of January. February used to be very scenic in Amritsar. The flower of February – Delia – now makes its entrance in the month of March.

After Lohri, in January, entire Amritsar enjoys flying the kites. This continues till Basant Panchmi, the spring festival. And by this time the colour of Halwa, a sweet dish for breakfast, also changes. The Gur Ka Halwa is now Basanti Halwa. Gur Ka Halwa is made of jaggery, while the Basanti Halwa is made of sugar. Interestingly, one can observe a change in people's behaviour as well. People, across religion and caste, enjoy festivals of the month. Basant Panchmi and Shivratri are very important festivals. These have religious importance.

Celebration of Shivratri is a must-see event at Shivala Bhaiyan. Shivala Bhaiyan temple is the main Shivalay (temple of God Shiva) in Amritsar. Many Hindus in Amritsar are Shiva worshippers. On the day of Basant Panchmi, one can visit Cheharta Sahib Gurudwara. It is celebrated beautifully there. Cheharta Sahib is in remembrance of the sixth Guru of Sikhs, Guru Hargobind Ji. There is a two-day fair at Cheharta Sahib which has a rustic feel to it. People especially with their newly born children visit for thanksgiving to this Gurudwara and drink pious water from a very old well in the premises of Cheharta Sahib. If somebody is visiting Amritsar around Basant Panchmi, he/she must go to this fair. It is on the way to Wagah Border.

Festivity in the month
On Basant Panchami children can be seen flying kites. The shops are open. Festivity is in the air. There is a reading of

Sukhmani Sahib in homes of Amritsaris. It is a part of Guru Granth Sahib and is believed to bring happiness to the family.

Valentine's Day is celebrated with equal enthusiasm in Amritsar. Amritsaris essentially need reasons to celebrate the day. Valentine's Day is just one more added reason.

It is not limited to the younger generation. People in their later years of life can be seen as equally excited about Valentine's Day. The city has something to itself which gives reasons to explore life for everyone. There are many clubs hosting musical evenings on Valentine's Day. One cannot ignore the fact that February 14th has the kind of whether one needs to enjoy Amritsar. Cold breeze has surrounded you. Romance is in the air. Amritsar is the perfect city to experience Valentine's Day!

Flower clubs in the city
The city has many flower clubs. Amritsar has a large population of people who have a good time to explore the beauty of life. The spring season is the time when the members of flower clubs meet and discuss flowers. One such group is 'Delia'. Members, including the amateur flower enthusiasts, meet and spend hours discussing gardening. Unlike a metropolis, Amritsar houses have gardens. So, people can afford the luxury of gardening.

Essentially, February is a very sweet month. Before this month, people are hiding away in their houses because of the extreme cold. This is the month when everybody comes out in their lawns, is busy in festivities while cherishing the Sun!

MARCH
Phagun-Chet

Chet(i) govind(u) arâdhîai hovai anand ghanâ.
Sant janâ mil(i) pâîai rasnâ nâm(u) bhanâ.

(In the month of Chet, the blossoming orchards all around give pleasure to the mind. If we remember God, it will add to the existing pleasure making it a spiritual experience.)

March marks the beginning of the new season, winter has just said goodbye to the city while summer is just a few steps away. Weather is pleasant, it is arguably the best time to see the city in its glory. As per the lunar calendar, Chet is the first month of the year. Another time for celebrations in this vibrant city. Weather is great, hence the time for indulging in some lip-smacking delicacies too.

The month of Holi
March is all about Holi, not only in Amritsar but all across north India. Unlike the rest of the country, here the Holi festival is celebrated at night as well. As per tradition in Amritsar, Holi is celebrated for seven days. For the last four days are celebrated with much enthusiasm. Major shops in the market are closed and fewer people are seen on the streets. Most of the them prefer to spend time with their families and friends.

Interestingly, people in Amritsar are known to have a good sense of humour. And the festival of Holi gives them the opportunity to explore it more. If you are here during this time, you'll find people dressed funnily, or people assembled for fake baraat or wedding procession. This is one of the many scenes of Holi in Amritsar which has started vanishing. The city has become modern for good, but with modern times we do lose some things, things that were eternal part of the culture before and people did wait for it.

In the earlier times, The Golden Temple had its own way of celebrating the festival of Holi. For seven days, flowers where showered in the temple, just outside the Akal Takht Sahib, in the evenings. People used to assemble outside the Akal Takht Sahib, sitting in a Sangat, (assembly of people) and enjoy the shower of flowers along with kewda (fragrance). Since the last two decades, this tradition has stopped.

In present times, Holi is essentially celebrated for two days. The actual day of Holi and the day after is called Hola Mohalla. Hola Mohalla is celebrated at night in the Golden Temple. On this day, during the procession of Shri Guru Granth Sahib Ji in the late evening, people assembled outside the Akal Takht Sahib, throw flowers, rose water and fragrance on Sangat. Hola is celebrated in the night time for almost two hours.

The biggest Hindu temple in Amritsar is Durgyana Temple. Holi is celebrated for three days in Durgyana Temple in the form of Raag Sabha. Raag Sabha is a very prestigious classical music gathering which has been organised for more than a century at the Durgyana Temple. Musical legends from across India and from various generations have performed at the Raag Sabha.

Holi has one bitter memory in its fold. It is said that communal riots of Indo-Pak partition had started on the day of Holi in 1947.

The Liquor Festival
Though not very popular among locals, March is known for an extremely interesting fair or mela, called Sharaab Ka Mela. The festival occurs in the first week of March, approximately 18 kilometres away from the city. People from all walks of life offer a bottle of whiskey at the shrine of Baba Rode Shah. All the whiskey received is mixed, and given back to the people. This is where the class barrier diminishes. A rich man's expensive whiskey is mixed with a poor man's whiskey, and they both consume the mixed version.

The after effects can be seen from 3 kilometres from the shrine. People can be found in the lush green farmlands, on the roads, not in their senses – still trying to make sense of their lives.

Food thoughts in March
The month of March is known for Phirni. Although it is now available throughout the year but traditionally, it was only consumed during the festival of Holi. A true Amritsari will not consume Phirni after April, despite it being available. After April Amritsaris shift to Rasmalai, another sweet dish made of dairy.

The best Phirni is available at the Ahuja Sweets, near the Hindu College. And if you are already at the Ahuja Sweets, there is no reason to avoid their wonderful Lassi. Interestingly, Lassi is not consumed throughout the year. People start drinking it in and around Holi. And it continues to dominate the beverage section in Amritsar till the time it starts to rain.

APRIL
Chet-Vaisakh

Vaisâkh(i) dhîran(i) kio(n) vâdîâ jinnâ prem bichhoh(u).
Her(i) sâjan(u) purakh(u) visâr(i) kai lagî mâyâ dhoh(u).

(Vaisâkh brings day of desires and expectations for every one. Those who have absence of love for God in their heart, how can such a person achieve patience?)

With April, summer has officially entered the city. April, May and June are the summer months in this part of geography. India summers aren't very pleasant, though April isn't very harsh. In Amritsar, summers aren't all that bad. The season welcomes the most loved fruit, mango. It is arguably, the most loved fruit although there is no evidence to support that claim. Take a walk around the city and you'll see people enjoying mangoes.

The month of Vaisakhi
The thirteenth day of April is celebrated as the day of Vaisakhi, which is also the first day of the month of Vaisakh. Once in 5-7 years, the Vaisakhi comes on the fourteenth day, which is not considered auspicious in this part of the country.

Vaisakhi is a symbol of harvesting crops in Punjab. However, with shifts in seasons, the actual harvesting does not take place on April 13. Earlier the farmers would cut the wheat on this day. But now the wheat is generally not ready by this time. However, the festival has its cultural significance.

The newly born children are taken to the Golden Temple on the day of Vaishakhi, as the day is considered auspicious. The ritual is called 'Paani Chakhana', where the child tastes the pious water from the Sarovar (the holy pond) of the Golden Temple. The water is taken in a bowl with flower, which is generally rose. The adults make it a point to take a dip inside the Sarovar at the Golden Temple on the day of Vaisakhi. The day of Vaisakhi at the Golden Temple sees an enormous rush of people not only from Amritsar but from faraway lands. It is generally very difficult to take a dip in the pond due to the rush.

The infamous historical event of Jallianwala Bagh, which triggered the freedom movement in India, happened on the day of Vaisakhi in the year 1919 at Amritsar. Jallianwala Bagh

which used to be a public garden stretched over an area of 7 acres, with walls covering all of its sides, is a stone's throw away from Golden temple. It is now a national memorial. More than 1000 people died in this massacre due to open fire by British troops on a gathering of more than 25000 people. This Vaishakhi is remembered as the Khooni Vaisakhi - a bloody Vaisakhi.

Vaisakhi of 1978 is also remembered as Khooni Vaisakhi. 16 people were killed in the communal clashes on this day in the ensuing violence. This incident is considered to be a starting point in the events leading to Operation Blue Star and the 1980s insurgency in Punjab. However, with the blessings of Guru Ram Dass Ji on the city, Amritsaris have overcome such tragedies and are flourishing better than before.

Food thoughts in April
While Firni is the sweet of Holi, Imarti is the sweet of Vaisakhi. It has been a tradition to eat Imarti with Samosa on the day of Vaisakhi in Amritsar. The best Imarti can be found at Goenka Sweets, in Katra Ahluwalia.

Mutton is best enjoyed in the month of April because of it's not-so-harsh nature. In the summers, because temperatures soar high, mutton dishes are not recommended. However, if you still want to have it, there are myriad of places where you can order it, such as Sundar Meat Shop. Earlier, it used to be in the walled city of Amritsar, but now it can be found on the Maqbool Road. Another place serving great Mutton delicacies is Mohan Meat Shop. It is inside Gilwali Gate. You can easily miss this joint if you are unaware of the good food it serves. Another place for good Mutton is Prakash Meat Shop, which was earlier situated in the vicinity of the Golden Temple. It has now shifted to Maqbool Road in the new city of Amritsar. Another local's favourite is Adarsh Meat Shop in Ranjit Avenue. There is another place for good Mutton in Amritsar but it isn't easily accessible. If you know any Amritsari, then he/she can take you to Jahajgarh, which is the transport area in Amritsar. This place is known for serving amazing roasted Mutton.

For vegetarians, the options are as much. In summers Amritsaris enjoy their chaat-papri at Mathurawala in Lawrence Road. Another loved place is Brijwasi Chaat in Ranjit Avenue.

One can think about the number of words dedicated to food alone while talking about Amritsar. It is said that at any given time half of Amritsar is cooking food, while the other half is eating.

MAY
Vaisakh-Jeth

Her(i) Jeth(i) jurhandâ lorhîai, jis agai sabh(i) nivann(i).
Her(i) sajan dâvan(i) lagiâ(n) kisai n deî bann(i).

(If we keep attached with the hem of the Lord-friend, it shall remove all fear of death.)

The summers are harsh in the month of May in Amritsar. The heat waves are strong during this time but as worrisome as it may sound, the worst doesn't hit the city till next month.

A morning walk in the Company Garden
The morning walks in Company Garden are beautiful. Located adjacent to Lawrence Road and Queen's Road, it is spread over an area of approximately 15 acres. Often referred to as the 'Lungs of Amritsar', this place was earlier known by the name, Rambagh Gardens. It was the summer garden of Maharaja Ranjit Singh who was the only Sikh King of ancient times. If you are here in Amritsar for a few days, this place should be on your list. Besides obvious health benefits of walking, the garden attracts people who wish to

spend some amazing time with their friends. The best thing about this place is that it is loved by retirees, elderly, working professionals, kids and housewives, equally. The behaviour and lifestyle of the people of Amritsar is best experienced here. If you are here at 7 in the morning, it is most likely that you'll see people laughing and cracking jokes with each other while enjoying the game of bridge. There are some melodious (and some not so much) singers who you are going to see and hear at the park. After you take 3-4 rounds of the park, you'll get the gist. Later, the addebazi shifts to Gyani Tea Stall, which is very close to the garden. Amritsaris love to binge on kachori, omelette and gulab jamun. To start a day at such a place is something everyone would love.

A period of break
There isn't much to do in May in Amritsar so it kind of provides a break to Amritsaris from all the hustle and bustle. However, the clubs here make sure that people don't get too used to the silence around and organise musical concerts through out the month.

The Amritsar Club, which is situated inside the Company Bagh, organises 'May Queen' competition during this time. Women from all across the city participate in it very enthusiastically. The participants aren't professional models and come from different walks of life. These participants are, of course, who's who of Amritsar and members of The Amritsar Club, which is one of the oldest clubs in the city established by the Britishers in colonial India. The other two clubs are The Lumsden Club and The Service Club. All these clubs have limited access.

Nowadays, lots of pubs and nightclubs have mushroomed in the city. Ranjit Avenue is one such area which is full of trendy cafes, pubs, fine dine restaurant, a food street and what not. People are seen having their evening drinks and snacks sitting in their cars, which is obviously against the law. Ranjit Avenue C Block market area has become a busy food street over the years.

Places of Art
Amritsar has contributed immensely in the field of arts and there are a few places worth mentioning. Punjab Naatshala is one beautiful place for theatre performances. It is just opposite historic Khalsa College. Punjab Naatshala was founded by Jatinder Brar, in the year 1998. This place has, since then, provided a platform to many artists to enhance their creativity. Theatre groups from all over the country and also from Pakistan come and perform here regularly. The people of Amritsar visit this place for theatrical experiences. Weekend shows are always houseful.

The other place of interest is The Indian Academy of Fine Arts, commonly called The Art Gallery. The place is near the Novelty Sweets at the Lawrence Road. This is the hub of artists in Amritsar, famous poets, photographers, theatre personalities and other artists are members of the academy. A heart surgeon can be seen playing the saxophone, an academician can be seen painting, or a chartered accountant can be seen sculpting in The Art Gallery.

JUNE
Jeth-Harh

Âsârh(u) tapandâ tis(u) lagai Her(i) nah(u) na jinnâ pâs(i).
Jagjîwan purakh(u) tiâg(i) kai, mânas sandî âs.

(The heat of Âsârh month is felt by those human beings whose heart is empty of the memory of almighty and for those who depend upon human beings for everything in their lives.)

The days have gotten longer in June. In Gurbani, the months of Jeth and Harh are referred to as the months of peak summer. The days seem never-ending, more often than not the days end by 8 pm in the evening. The weather during this time gets hot and humid and temperature can go as high as 48 degree Celsius. The city gets too hot to get outside during this time of the month.

It was in the month of June that the fifth Guru of the Sikh religion, Guru Arjan Dev Ji, who created the Golden Temple, was martyred.

Shaheedi Mela

Jeth Sudi Chauth, popularly known as Shaheedi Mela, is the city's way of celebrating the legacy of the Guru Arjan Dev Ji. It is also known by the name Chabeel wala Mela, which is now very popular throughout the country. However, there is no dedicated space for the celebration of this festival. The entire city pays homage to their beloved Guru Arjan Dev Ji by serving cold beverage to the people. Every corner of the city is turned into a Chabeel, a place where one can take sweet water.

Gurudwara Ram Sar Sahib, dedicated to Guru Arjan Dev Ji, is one of the five ponds (sarovar) in Amritsar. The other sarovars are Bibek Sar, Kaul Sar, Santhok Sar and Amrit Sar. The main Chabeel is organised at Gurudwara Ram Sar Sahib, which is located right next to Gurudwara Shaheedan Sahib near Chatiwind Gate. Shaheedan Sahib is the second most visited Gurudwara after the Golden Temple. It is at Gurudwara Ram Sar Sahib that the Guru Granth Sahib, the holy book of the Sikh religion, is printed. During Shaheedi Mela people are served sweet water along with Ghugni, which is a dish made of chickpeas. The day of celebration is also called the Guru Purab, the festival of the Guru. Since everyone can't be served in a single day, Chabeel is organised at various places for the entire month by different people.

It must be noted that there is a bigger message hidden behind all these festivities. Guru Arjan Dev Ji was murdered by the Mughals ruthlessly by putting him on a huge burning pan. It is believed that Guru Arjan Dev Ji did not utter anything during this time except, "Tera bhaana meetha laage." (Whatever the Almighty is doing, it is for good.) So, instead of mourning his death, people decided to make it a point to help others by serving them cold and sweet water, irrespective of their religion. This is to spread the message of peace.

If you are entering the city on the day of Chabeel, people will stop your car and hand you sweet water. Not taking the water due to any reason isn't well received during this day.

Operation Blue Star
Guru Purab of 1984 is still remembered as a black day in the recent history of Amritsar and India. Operation Blue Star was carried out by then Central government on the day of Guru Purab in June 1984, between June 1 and June 8. It was the codename of the military action carried out to remove religious leader Jarnail Singh Bhindranwale and his followers from the Golden Temple. The act was hugely criticised as it affected a large number of devotees who were trapped inside the Golden Temple while this action was taken. This amount of fear among people was last seen during the time of partition riots in 1947. The confrontation between Army and the followers of Bhindranwale went on for three days. During this time, over 576 people were killed, including 83 soldiers. Finally, when the Akal Takht was blown away with the help of an army tank, the confrontation came to an end. This remains a black day in the history of Amritsar. The month of June thus remains in people's conversation forever. It initiated an era of terrorism in Punjab, which continued for another decade. Since 1984, all the shops including the shopping malls of the entire city remain closed on the day of 6th June in the memory of Operation Blue star.

The month of vacation
As for entire north India, the month of June is the time for welcoming the summer vacations. Amritsaris love to travel to the mountains when they have time. One of the most popular haunts for them is Mussoorie. Some of the others include Dalhousie and McLeodgunj, which are not too far from Amritsar.

Food thoughts in June
Lassi is the favourite drink during this month and throughout the year. Many Amritsaris start their day by having Poori in breakfast followed by homemade Lassi. Not many milk products are used in the month because of the summer season. Best pooris are available at local favourites, Novelty Sweets, Kanha Sweets and Kanhaiya Sweets, located at Lawrence Road.

One of the most popular evening snacks of Amritsar is Kulcha Chole. It is quite different from what the rest of the north India knows about Kulcha. It looks like a pita bread and is served with chanas (chickpeas) poured over it. Non-vegetarians can get a mutton combo too. Faluda Kulfi at Queens Road, near Crystal Restaurant is a must eat in the summer evenings. Some of the other favourites of Amritsaris are homemade dana, malai rabri and doodh soda. Another popular sweet that people relish in summer is badana.

Monsoon enters the city by the end of June. One can sense the drop in temperature and the city looks much greener during this time. Monsoon is like a theatrical show in the city with elements of drama in the city.

JULY
Harh-Sawan

Sâvan(i) sarsî kâmanî charn kamal sio(n) piâr(u).
Man(u) tan rattâ sach rang(i) iko nâm(u) adhâr(u).

(As everything becomes green and full of life with the rain in the month of Savan, so does that human beings become full of life who attaches her/his mind with the holy feet of the Lord.)

It is in the month of July that monsoon officially arrives in the city. People get a relief from scorching heat as the clouds play hide and seek with the sun. Weather gets pleasant and inviting, the locals love to indulge in activities they were blocking themselves from in the past months. Monsoon dictates the lifestyle in the month.

The houses in the walled city of Amritsar are so small that there is no proper ventilation. Old houses are built in a manner that there is no gap between the two houses. Most of the rooftops have a shed of iron and steel called Mugh in Punjabi. This is to provide sunlight and ventilation in the

rooms. During monsoon, the water creates a sound when it falls on these Mughs. Even when there is little rain, the sound is amplified, and it gives a false sense of a heavy rainfall. This sound is the background music of monsoon in Amritsar. People have grown listening to it. It is part of the larger picture of the city's memory.

Monsoons are best enjoyed with Pakodas and Chai. The houses in Amritsar are, generally, bigger and has a verandah. So, everybody can enjoy monsoon equally.

Celebration of Saawein
The newlyweds celebrate Saawein in the month of Saawan (mid-July to mid-August). This is a beautiful celebration where you will see newlywed girls wearing jewellery made of Jasmine flowers (the flower of the month), in their bridal dresses. The Hindu girls will be seen mostly in Durgayana Temple, or sometimes even in the Golden Temple. The idea of the celebration is simply to have fun on Sundays. This may be one way for the new bride to strengthen her bonds with the new family members. Every Sunday in the month of Saawan hundreds of brides has gathered in the Durgayana temple. The sight is simply beautiful. If somebody is travelling to Amritsar during this period, he/she must not miss this sight.

There is another wonderful thing about Amritsar. The Hindus celebrate the Sikh festival with equal enthusiasm. And the Sikhs celebrate the Hindu festival with equal joy. And the festivals which do not belong to Sikhs or Hindus, are celebrated with more enthusiasm by both! In the end, Amritsaris are looking for a reason to celebrate life.

Food thoughts in July
Monsoons are incomplete without an evening session of Pakode and Chai, along with the evening Kulcha. This

Amritsari kulcha is unique to the city and no neighbouring city has been able to replicate it perfectly. People say it as has something to do with the water of the city.

During monsoon people generally, avoid dinners at home. Talya (fried vegetables) is a local dish which is best enjoyed during monsoon. It is available everywhere in the city. People indulge in Talya along with the Kulcha.

The other favourite food of the season is the Maalpura. It is available to the people from the month of July till December. It's form keeps changing from month to month and season to season. In Sawan and Bhadon – July & August, and mid-September – Maalpura will be served with Chasni, the sweet sugary syrup. After that, people discard the syrup and start consuming it dry. The best Maalpura is available at Mehar Halwaai, situated at Chaurasti Attari in Guru Bazaar. It has been serving delicious Maalpura for many decades. Guru Bazaar is a very old jeweller's market in Amritsar. If you are visiting this market, do try chicken and mutton biryani.

There is a posh residential area in Amritsar called Green Avenue. There is a local market there where a person sells bread pakoras in a small cart. It's called by the name Om Chat Centre and it has been there since decades. Popular all over the city, the taste of these bread pakoras remains with you for a long, long time. The seller has a great understanding of the economics and is quite interesting to discuss issues with him. As per him, if he is gaining profit of his small cart of bread pakora, the city is prospering and if he is loss then the city is headed towards depression, simple enough? He isn't totally wrong, a great number of businessmen live the area and if they aren't spending much of street food how can an entire city enjoy the luxury of these lip-smacking pakoras.

By the end of July, the mango season will be over. To culminate the season of mango, people throw a lot of mango themed parties in different parts of the city. These parties are a part of the city's culture. People invite their friends and family for these parties where every dish from starter to the main delicacy is made of mango. Amritsaris experiment with food. In winters they will be organising fish themed parties.

Chronology of mango is very interesting. Mango is rightfully called the king of fruits. The mango season starts with safeda in the month of May, followed by langda. Langda, after staying for almost two weeks, is replaced by dusehri. And finally, shahad ki kuppi and chausa bring the mango season to an end in July.

AUGUST
Sawan-Bhaadon

Bhâduey bharm(i) bhulânîa, dûjai lagâ heyt(u).
Lakh sîgâr banâiâ kâraj(i) nâhî keyt(u).

(As a man feels restless in the humid and sultry weather of Bhâdaon month, similarly he who falls in love with someone other than God, wanders and goes astray from the path of life. He may do many kinds of makeup and ornamentations, but all that is worthless.)

The effect of monsoon diminishes in the month of August and weather gets very humid after that.

This period is called Chaumasa, it is the period which has features of the four seasons. The days can surprise you; it can be hot, pleasant, cold or humid, this month is full of wonders. It is during this month that the city prepares for festivities yet again. This is month of Rakshabandhan or rakhi, followed by Independence Day. August onwards, the weather starts getting more pleasant with temperature getting down day by day until winter arrives.

Festival of Tiyaan
The festival of Tiyaan is celebrated with much enthusiasm and vigor in Amritsar and the entire state of Punjab. One of the best things about this festival is that it is celebrated by both Hindus and Sikhs. The festival isn't bound by religion and is basically a community festival which had a social significance since olden times. It is normally celebrated in third week of Bhadon (late August).

Earlier, during Tiyaan, married women used to visit their maayka (their parents' home). All the women visiting their parents' house used to gather in a common place which could be a farmland or any other common place of the village and gossip about their husbands and in laws. These gossip sessions later gave birth to folk songs or 'Boliyan' with Giddha, a Punjabi dance form. The songs are famous for their humour and married women of all ages used to participate in it. The frustration and hardship of day to day life thus used to diminish. Men on the other hand used to keep themselves busy by playing kabaddi or just chatting amongst themselves. In the evening, after eating kheer-pura the women would promise to be back the next year and leave their houses again.

In present times, women visit their maayka quite often. Also, there is no culture of going out in the fields and sing songs. However, Tiyaan is celebrated with enthusiasm. Women gather in their maaykas on any one day in August along with other married women in the family over lunch. It is a very common sight in Amritsar. Many houses host this family get together and invite their daughters and granddaughters along with their children.

Celebration of Rakhi
Rakhi is called Rakhri in Punjabi language. This is yet another festival which has cultural roots and not religious. You can see most of the communities enjoying this festival. That's the beauty of Indian festivals they are all secular in nature. There are many stories about the origin of the festival of Rakhi or Rakshabandhan. It celebrates the love between brothers and sisters. However, girls who do not have brothers would tie Rakhi on the hands of their cousins, uncle or even father. Essentially, it is celebration of trust and faith.

On the day of Rakhi, Amritsaris go to Gurudwara Shaheedan Sahib and tie symbolic Rakhi to Baba Deep Singh Ji. The Gurudwara was created in memory of Baba Deep Singh Ji, who was martyred in eighteenth century, protecting the honour of the Golden Temple. Baba Deep Singh Ji is revered in Amritsar; he is the ultimate protector of the city. Gurudwara Shaheedan Sahib is one of the most visited Gurudwaras by Amritsaris.

The memory of August 1947 – Partition of India
August is incomplete without the mention of the biggest tragedy Amritsar has witnessed in modern times, the partition of India and Pakistan. Lahore and Amritsar were two of the most important cities in Punjab region of the undivided India. Both the cities of Lahore and Amritsar had deeper ties. The partition brought an end to centuries old bond between the two cities.

There are many people in Amritsar who have seen the era of partition. For days and months, the city witnessed riots. Before the partition, Amritsar had a significant Muslim population, the partition changed the colour of the map. Most of the Muslims either fled to Pakistan or died in the riots. Millions of people were directly affected by the partition.

The population of Muslims in Amritsar has grown smaller with time. The anger among people due to partition has died down and people are curious to know about the city of Lahore but political restrictions do not allow them to do so. It is very difficult to visit Lahore from Amritsar despite the fact that the two cities are hardly 40 kilometers away from each other.

Wagah Border
For the last few years, on 14th August people from both the cities - Amritsar and Lahore - assemble at Wagah Border and do candle vigil, which is sometimes followed by a music concert on the Indian side. These days Wagah Border has become a major tourist attraction and draws a large number of tourists. The flag retreat ceremony from both the countries before the sunset every day is witnessed by a large number of people every day. People from both the countries can be seen waving at each other. The ceremony doesn't stop even during the days of high tension between the two countries.

Interestingly, the place is known as Wagah Border but Wagah is in Pakistan side of the border. In the Indian side of the border, it is called Attari. The border is named after Sardar Sham Singh Attari who was the chief in the great Sikh army of Maharaja Ranjit Singh. The history is filled with the stories of bravery of these brave and fearless Sikhs who had defeated the army of marauders who were attacking India from the west. Important government offices, such as immigration and customs are located at Attari.

Food thoughts in August
Owing to the humid weather in the month of August, people love to indulge in sweet delicacies.

Maalpura, shahi tukra and kheer are loved by one and all. People to make shahi tukras at home and call it Meethe Toast (a sweetened toast bread).

SEPTEMBER
Bhadon - Assu

Asun(i) prem umâhrhâ kio(n) milîai Her(i) jâey.
Man(i) tan(i) piâs darsan ghânî, Koî ân(i) milâvai mâey.

(After the humid and sultry weather of Bhadon month, the sweet weather of Assu is creating much longing in the mind to see and meet my Lord husband.)

September has arrived in the timeless city. This is the month of Bhadon and Assu. There is a saying for the month of Assu, it gives you can idea of the weather of the month, Assu put syala, Diney garmi te raati pala. 'Syal' is the period of winter and 'put' means son. This roughly translates like this, the month of Assu is the son of Syal. And days will be hot while nights will be cold. Thus, the weather will not be as harsh as the winters but will have its characteristics. This is the start of early winters, people stop using air conditioners by this time. This is a beautiful time to experience Amritsar.

The month of September kick starts the wedding season of the year which will continue till February. There is no culture of matching the janam-patri, (natal chart), or waiting for the perfect muhurat (auspicious day) amongst the Sikh community for the wedding purposes. Usually weekends are considered to be apt for the wedding ceremonies.

This is also the time when Navratras starts. There is no fixed date for Hindu festivals. It depends upon the lunar calendar. Navratras can fall anytime between September and November. There will be enough festivals throughout the month to keep the people occupied.

Navratras in Amritsar
Navratras is a very auspicious 9-day period for Hindus and it holds a special place for the Sikhs too. Over the years, people have developed their own understanding of religion. Followers of Sikhism and Hinduism have many shared beliefs in Amritsar and other places. Amritsar is a good example to understand this phenomenon. Many people give up non-vegetarian food during Navratras.

The most fascinating part of Navratras is the Langooron Wala Mela organised in the Durgayana Temple in Amritsar. Inside the Durgayana Temple, there is temple called Bada Hanuman Temple. It is believed that when Sita, wife of Lord Ram, was serving her period of exile with her children, Luv and Kush, she stayed at this place. When Luv and Kush stopped the Ashwamedh Yagya Rath of Lord Ram, Hanuman went to talk to Luv and Kush. The two brothers, then captured Hanuman, and tied him with rope a to a tree. It is believed that tree is still at this place, and it is where the Bada Hanuman Temple is mounted. The temple is highly revered by the Hindus. It is believed that Lord Hanuman listens to the people in pain. Many married couples who are unable to have a child visit the temple and make a wish. Parents pray to the lord and commit to him that if their wish is granted, they will make their child a langoor during Navratas. The child will pe a part of Lord Hanuman's army during Navratras. The children wear a red jacket with stars on them, and a cap which makes them look like a monkey. For seven days, the parents would take their child to the temple. On the eighth day, there is a big celebration and the festival concludes with fireworks on Dussehra or Vijay Dashmi. Professional groups would perform as monkeys during the mela. It is a wonderful and fun thing to watch.

Memories of 1965
The mention of 1965 brings back the memories of intense war between India and Pakistan witnessed by the city of Amritsar. Amritsar became a battleground. Many old Amritsaris recount their story of the war.

Tension between India and Pakistan had reached its zenith in September 1965. The situation escalated to the point of a full-fledged war. Amritsar witnessed the largest tank battle in military history since World War II. Armies from both the countries were already fighting the battle in Jammu and Kashmir sector. As per reports, Pakistan was losing the battle. It was then both the countries decided to declare ceasefire on September 23, 1965. But fate had other plans.

Suddenly Amritsaris saw fighter planes in the open sky. It took time for people to realize that Pakistan has attacked India. It was an air attack. Indian forces took charge of the situation. A fierce battle was fought. Many soldiers died from both the countries. Sadly, as many as hundred civilians from Amritsar also died in this war, when Pakistan dropped bombs on Amritsar.

Many planes also crashed in Amritsar. People recount how Amritsaris went to collect the debris as souvenirs for themselves. Pakistan also attacked India on land. But Indian forces fought bravely. They were able to not only stop the Pakistani forces to enter India but got their tanks and buses as souvenirs of war. Amritsaris came in numbers to see these souvenirs of war. One of the war souvenirs, a Pakistani Patton tank, is put on display near the Gobindgarh Fort in the city.

The war was a tragedy. Sadly, Amritsar has witnessed many wars from the time it was founded by Guru Ram Das Ji. But the city has come back to life, always.

Food thoughts in September
September is the best time to indulge in the wondrous Amritsari Kulcha. Although kulchas are available all year round but due to amazing weather during this month, people tend to enjoy it more. Interestingly, Amritsari Kulcha has become a sort of a rage across India. It is now available in every part of the country. Many people have tried to replicate the recipe but they aren't very successful.

There are few places where one can get the best Kulchas in Amritsar. Kulwant Singh Kulchewala near the Golden Temple is where one can get a better Kulcha. As a matter of fact, the best Kulchas are not available in any restaurant, but on the streets. If you get confused at any point of time, ask an Amritsari and he will lead you to the best kulcha you'll ever have.

This is also the best time to introduce you to Kesar Da Dhaba. Chances are that you would have already heard this name if you have ever visited Amritsar. This is the place Amritsari are in love with. A century old vegetarian restaurant, this is the most visited food haven in Amritsar.

This is where one can get the authentic Amritsari Thali and food. After having a scrumptious thali at Kesar, one must eat their Angoori Rasmalai. And do not forget to take a tour of their open kitchen.

Kachoris are important part of Amritsari food culture. During this period Kachoris are given more attention. There is a food protocol for Kachoris – an unsaid rule followed by the Amritsaris. In the mornings Kachoris are supposed to be eaten with Halwa, whereas in the evenings people eat it with Chana.

OCTOBER
Assu-Katak

Katik(i) karm kamâvaney dos(u) na kâhû jog(u).
Parmesar te bhuliân viâpan(i) sabhey rog.

(If one remains separated from his/her Lord husband in the beautiful season of the month of Katik, then it is the result of one's own deeds.)

The month starts with Assu, which is one of the most pleasant periods in the year. The city is walking away from the summers, and by the end of this month, in the lunar month of Katak, there will be cold days. Evenings are beautiful. This is the period when you want to go out of the house in the evening, take a stroll around the city, and walk back to your home – holding hand of your loved one.

October is probably the most happening month of the year when it comes to festivals. The entire month is full of festivity. People are in a festive mood. We will have Dussehra, followed by Karwachauth. Dhanteras makes an entry. Diwali comes next. Then there will be Vishwakarma Puja. And in the end there will be Bhai Dooj, commonly called Tikka in the Punjab region. These are bigger and smaller festivals of the month.

Diwali in Amritsar
There is a beautiful saying for Diwali in Amritsar. 'Daal roti ghar di, Diwali Amritsar di', which loosely translates to - one can get the best food at home, and best Diwali is seen in Amritsar. All across India Diwali is celebrated with great enthusiasm. But in Amritsar this enthusiasm is clubbed with the beautiful celebration at the Golden Temple.

Celebration at Golden Temple is so beautiful that people from far away places throng the city to witness it. The Golden Temple is beautifully lit throughout the year. But on the day of Diwali it illuminates with Diyas and light. It is an annual ritual for both Sikhs and Hindus to visit The Golden Temple on Diwali eve or on the day of festival. Imagine thousands of diyas dancing to the tunes of the festival of lights – this is that day, at its poetic beauty. Everybody takes a dip in the holy sarovar in the temple premises. It is considered auspicious to do so. At times it becomes difficult to take a dip in the pond. In such case, people take water in their hands from the pond and sprinkle it on their body for five times. This is a common sight in Diwali and also on the day of Vaisakhi.

On the day of Diwali, the entire market area of old Amritsar is decorated with colours and light. The night market adds to the beauty. The markets – Hall Bazar, Paschim wala Bazar, Namakmandi, and few others are open throughout the night. One can see sweets-towers in front of the sweets shops in the walled city of Amritsar. This is a very Diwali specific scene in the old market area. Everybody is seen buying sweets and small gifts for somebody or other.

At night, Diwali Puja ritual is done. Sikh families in Amritsar also perform Aarti with recitation of Gurbani in their prayer rooms at homes fondly called Baba ji da Room - Baba ji is synonyms of their Gurus. Everyone in the family assemble at Baba ji's Room and do prayers. After prayers the eldest member of the family distribute money to the rest of the family. After playing with crackers, there are long innings of gambling at homes with friends and families. Truly speaking, gambling sessions starts around three weeks before Diwali and concludes on Diwali night. Amritsaris, whether man or woman, across all ages participate in gambling for fun.

Sweets in the market, diyas on the streets, and crackers in the sky – this is the visual summary of Amritsar on this particular day.

Karwachauth in Amritsar
Nine days before Diwali, the city enjoys the celebration of Karwachauth. Karwachauth is a Punjabi festival which is now celebrated throughout India thanks to the romantic depiction of the festival in Bollywood films.

During Karwachauth women pray for the long lives of their husbands. Women fast on the day of Karwachauth. And they end their fast only after seeing full moon and their husband together in the evening. There is one more ritual attached with this festival. Women visit maaykas - their mother's home and bring Meeti Mathi- a kind of sweet dessert as a gift for their mother in laws. These token of gift is called Baya. Such small gestures on festival day increases the bond between two families.

Amritsar knows how to make the most out of any festival. The idea is to have a grand celebration. At least four days before the festival one can see entire Lawrence Road with women outside every shop getting their hands decorated with Mehndi, or as some call it the Henna art. Many Mehndi artists from Rajasthan travel to Amritsar to earn during the Karwa Chauth period. Women from diverse backgrounds – rich and poor – young and old – sit together, while the Mehndi artists show their creativity on their hands. This has been part of the culture for years.

Food thoughts in October
No month is complete without food thoughts in Amritsar. The month of October has so much to offer because of the festivals of the month. One must try Jalebis at Amritsar. There are few amazing Jalebi options in the city. Gurdasram Jalebiwala in the old city at Katra Ahluwalia, near the Golden Temple, makes some amazing Jalebi. The shop is more than 60 years old. It is so famous that the adjoining street crossing is called Jalebiwala Chawk. Another favourite Jalebi place is the Sharma Jalebi in Lawrence Road. Their crisp Jalebis can add happiness to your life anytime! These Jalebi shops are so loved that whenever there is the slightest rainfall in the city, you can see numerous cars outside Sharma Jalebi, and numerous people outside Gurdasram Jalebiwala. Jalebis are part of the celebration called life.

To summarise the month of October, every Amritsari has gained at least two to three kilos of weight by the end of the month.

NOVEMBER
Katak - Maghar

Manghar(i) mâhey suhandîâ(n) Her(i) pir sang(i) baitharhîâh.
Tin kî sobhâ kiâ ganî je sâhib(i) melarhîâh.

(In the cold month of Manghar, those who are united with the master-Lord, their body and mind is always in a blooming state.)

Here it comes - November. And also winters have finally arrived. The joyous mood of people in the city is at its festive best. Diwali has just ended, but the celebrations in one form or other continues. The famous religious carnivals called Nagar Kirtans are just around the corner. The weather is at its best. Evenings are as beautiful as the days. Men wait for November to open their winter wardrobes. The fashion savvy people of Amritsar start wearing suits from the very beginning of November, though November is not very cold. The coats and suits shall again be re-packed in March.

The lunar month of Maghar starts mid November. Birth Anniversaries of the founder of the city Sri Guru Ram Dass ji, the fourth Sikh Guru and Guru Nanak Dev ji, the first Guru, normally falls in this month. Birth Anniversaries are respectfully called Gurupurab. Both the Gurupurabs sometimes falls in October as per the lunar calendar. But mostly they fall in November. Even Diwali sometimes falls in November.

Nagar Kirtan of Amritsar
The people of the city wait the whole year for the famous religious carnivals called the Nagar Kirtan. The Nagar Kirtan is observed one day before the Gurupurab. It starts from Golden Temple and ends at the same place after visiting the whole city for 5-6 hours. The procession of Nagar Kirtan include live performances of the martial art of Sikhs- Gatka. Parade by children with their school bands is an eye pleasing sight of the Nagar Kirtan. Singing of holy hymns by people of the city followed by the palki of Guru Granth Sahib, the holy scripture of the Sikhs. The palki is led by Panj Piare- the five Sikhs from different castes. They are appointed by the organizers of the Nagar Kirtan. In Sikh religion Guru Granth sahib is respected as the living Guru and Panj Piare- the five Sikhs is the symbol of the philosophy of Sikhism of equality without any caste bias.

Nagar Kirtans are observed three times in a year – twice in November for Guru Nanak Dev ji and Guru Ramdass Ji and once in January for Guru Gobind Singh ji- the tenth Guru of Sikhs. Thousands of Amritsaris take part in these carnivals every year to mark respect for their beloved Gurus.

A typical November Day
After the humid months of August, September and festivity of Diwali in October, people return to their morning walks at Company Gardens. Their desire to shed extra 4-5 kilos,

they have put on during festive months bring them here. The pleasant weather adds to the charm of the walkers.

After a good breakfast and equally good lunch, people can be seen napping at their shops in the afternoon. Amritsaris also have the luxury to visit their homes for lunch followed by a cat nap. The city is very small. Everything is at a small distance. So many people prefer to visit their homes for lunch.

Evenings are equally fun. Amritsaris have traditionally been fond of the street food. With the emergence of good restaurants, many people have started visiting restaurants as well. This cannot be a rule, but at least in November Amritsaris go out at least twice a week for dinner. Thanks to start-ups like Zomato and swiggy, they can also order the food to be consumed at home now.

Flora and fauna in November
Nature lovers of the city enjoy this month the most. It is the season of sowing flowers and vegetables. Since many people of the city enjoy the luxury of big houses, almost every house has a small kitchen garden and a lawn. Interestingly, People who do not keep lawns, still they hire part time gardeners to maintain their flower pots. The city is ready to welcome winter with flowers like Chrysanthemums, Camellia, Carnation, Daffodil, Poinsettia, Sweet Pea and many more. Small groups of people have many flower clubs in Amritsar to share their joy and love for flowers. For beginners it is a good forum to know about gardening. Winter vegetables like Cauliflower, Radish, Carrot, Sarson or Palak ka Sagh is also planted extensively by the residents in their backyards or pots.

The Social life
Social life of people of Amritsar is no less than any metro city of India. People have lots of time to spend afternoons

with their friends. Throughout the year, the three British era clubs- Amritsar Cub, Services Club and Lumsden club witness who's who of the city playing card games of Bridge and Rummy with their friends in the afternoon. While Lumsden Club and Service Club is occupied by men, many women can be seen playing their favourite card games at Amritsar club. On weekends small Mushiaras, poetry sessions, over evening drinks is a normal scene in the homes of Amritsaris. Poetry and storytelling sessions in an intimate gathering is very common. It is common to say that Amritsaris have a nag to enjoy life irrespective of their financial status.

Food thoughts in November
November is season of meat lovers. The best delicacies of Chicken and Mutton are tasted best in this season. It is very difficult to document best non-vegetarian eating joints in the city as the city is dotted with countless number of such outlets. if someone is really interested to taste some Amritsari non-vegetarian delicacies of the city, he should take along some one known in Amritsar. Bira Chicken and Makhan Fish at Majitha Road, food street at Ranjit Avenue, C- Block is equally famous with tourists and locals. The young crowd these days is more attracted towards the pubs, a new trend in the town. Gajar Ka Halwa and Jalebi are famous sweets of the month. Also, one can have the best chocolate brownies at cafe Bon Gateau and Bake-n-Beans located in the posh Ranjit Avenue area.

DECEMBER
Maghar-Poh

Pokh(i) tukhâr(u) na viâp-ee, kanth(i) miliâ Her(i) nâh(u).
Man(u) beydhiâ charnârbind, darsan(i) lagrhâ sâh(u).

(A human being who is attached with the Lord never feels the bite of the frost or extreme cold. Such a person is never impressed by the vagaries of evil forces and vices.)

The northern Indian belt witnesses severe cold in the months of December and January. December also brings an end to the modern calendar year. But does something really end in a timeless city? Not really.

Poh (starts mid-December) is a month when the days are relatively very short, and the nights are much longer. During the day when the Sun is still out there, Sun basking is the most common sight. The shopkeepers come out of their shops and enjoy the company of their old friends and the Sun.

There is an old saying for this period in Amritsar – 'Mahina Poh, bachan oh jede sovan-ge do', which means in the month of Poh only those survive who sleep as a couple. But of course even the single people do survive the cold waves of life. This is just a way of saying how intensely cold the weather is in this period of the year.

The old clubs in Amritsar – The Amritsar Club, The Service Club and The Lumsden Club - are always full with city people making the most of the winter months. During the evenings, one can see bonfire at every corner of the city.

Christmas and New Year celebrations
Christmas is one of the most enjoyed festivals in Amritsar. The Christian population stands at around two percent in Amritsar. But the entire city can be seen celebrating Christmas. This is majorly because Christmas is not seen as a religious festival. The year is coming to an end. People need one more reason to celebrate life. And voila! Here is the perfect festival to do so.

Various clubs organise baby shows, musical nights, game nights on this day. Christmas initiates the New Year's celebration. For the last seven nights of the year, everybody is partying. You do not need to go to a far away city to enjoy the year end. Amritsar is ready to welcome the new year with equal enthusiasm. Various clubs divide their celebration nights, so that there is no clash in celebration, and nobody misses one celebration because of the other.

Across all the restaurants in the city there is a fixed menu on 31st Of December because they cannot afford to serve A La Carte due to huge demand. Almost everybody is out celebrating the end of the year!

Not to anybody's surprise, even after partying all night, and celebrating night in the pubs and clubs of Amritsar, many people visit the Golden Temple to start the year on a positive note. The Golden Temple is the ultimate binding force in the city. People from various backgrounds come to the Golden Temple to seek blessings for the new beginnings.

Guru Gobind Singh ji's Gurupurab
In December, preparations start for celebrating the birth anniversary of the tenth Sikh Guru Shri Guru Gobind Singh ji. Around 21 days before the Gurupurab, small group of people from various residential colonies gather and do a round of the colony. They chant songs in praise of the Guru. These small processions are known as Prabhat Feris. The enthusiasm of these Prabhat Feris is not affected by biting cold of December. The faith in Guru gives this strength to its disciples.

Winter Vacations
Schools remain closed due to extreme cold from Twentieth day of December. Schools reopen in the second week of January next year. Being holidays, children prefer to remain in their cosy quilts making full use of winters. Sun basking is one of the most favourite pastimes of the people of the city. Even offices shift from rooms to the rooftops for the sun, temporarily.

Food thoughts in December
One can understand that celebration is a way of life in Amritsar. It is just not an occasional thing. People are celebrating life everyday. And somehow celebration is directly related to food in the city.

During December Pinni is the most favourite sweet in the city. Pinni is a sweet dessert made with desi Ghee, wheat flour, jaggery and almonds. Bansal Sweets on Lawrence road and Kanhaiya Sweets at Phoolon Wala Chawk make the best Pinni. Amritsaris love Pinni so much that they have different ways to eat this heavy dessert. Some eat it with egg, some mix it with milk. There are people who simply heat it and eat in the night. This is the guilty pleasure of Amritsaris in extreme winters.

Dodhi is a milk based drink which is most enjoyed in winters. It is a hot drink with Ghee, besan and lots of dry fruits. Dodhi keeps you warm, and it tastes amazing. People make this drink at home. This is not available at any shop. So, if one has to drink Dodhi, he/she needs to pamper an Amritsari friend!

Part 2
History written on the walls

The City That Is Amritsar

Sprawling along the east banks of the River Beas, Amritsar represents the essence of India. India sits gloriously in anybody's vision because of her tremendous cultural wealth, respect, divinity and hospitality. You can find all of this at one place in this timeless city of Amritsar. This is a city which is a repository of secular and national heritage. Life in Amritsar is energetic and colourful, fast-paced and chaotic. The simplistic charm of this city will win anyone's heart and the ever-hospitable local people are always willing to go out of their way to help you. It is this essence of the city that makes it spiritually lively and culturally colourful.

A deeper walk around the city will introduce you to its magnificent contrasting sides. Ambarsar has long been a city which has inherited values and principles from its deep-rooted traditional heritage and has also responded to the stimulus of modernity. While strolling through the walled city of Amritsar you will find yourself being welcomed into a maze of pedestrian alleys or galis. This tight tangle of the lanes will give you the vintage feels and introduce you to the rich cultural remnants of the city. It can be claustrophobic and crowded, but to venture into the most atmospheric part of the city is by far the most overwhelming experience. The city has witnessed its own share of modernity wave and is constantly evolving its way of life. You will come across a very different dynamic of Amritsar's city life. On one hand, on any given day, you will find the young crowd flocking to Ranjit Avenue. Parlours & boutiques, clubs, cafes & pubs are the new hangout places. The glittering malls have brought the market forces and commercialization to the city while on the other hand it keeps intact its cultural identity.

Amritsar is a thriving city in the Majha region of Punjab. The word Majha means the central or the heartland. It is situated in the middle of this historic Punjab region, hence the name. Historically, the city has been the part of the ancient Silk Route that connected China to Europe. Today if we look at this emerging power centre, we'll find that the economic fabric of this city is diverse. Trading and the service sector forms the backbone of the city. The waves of modernisation have paved its way for Amritsar to transcend its image of a holy city to a prime real estate investment destination. There are new buildings popping up in and around the city every other day. However, the new Amritsar and the old Amritsar appear to be two different cities with different characteristics of their own. The essence of the city is derived from its core, The Golden Temple.

Harmandir Sahib, The Golden Temple
The Golden Temple, the religious shrine for the Sikhs shines magnificently in its glory in the heart of the city. There is enough magic and tranquillity in the air to welcome the influx of devotees who throng the city from the country and abroad. With a dream to take that holy dip in the sarovar of the Gurudwara premises, lakhs of Sikhs and people from other religious beliefs, come from around the globe to Amritsar. The literal meaning of Amritsar is a pool of pious sweet water, it shows the importance of the Golden Temple and its sarovar. An interesting fact about Amritsar is that it was built and developed after the Golden Temple was constructed unlike other civilizations of the world where cities are built first, and religious places are built afterwards. Guru Granth Sahib, the holy scripture was placed in the temple in 1604. Since then, every morning at 4 am, it is religiously brought back to Harmandir Sahib from Akal Takht, its night-time abode. The Gurudwara looks exquisite at night. It glows stunningly, and the holy pond mesmerises the visitors with its glimmer and shine. The sight of the temple reflections in the dark rippling

water is a sight to behold. Several devotees spend hours sitting by the pond on the sparkling clean floor, admiring the architectural marvel that this temple is. Devotees are found touching the holy waters, creating ripples, making orange & black fish surface quickly and vanishes back in the dark with the same speed.

Today, the Golden Temple complex's architecture looks aesthetically consistent. However, it is the product of evolution over many centuries. This dazzling structure is a magnificent splendour and an admired masterpiece. It is rich and bright but not gaudy. The design of the temple exudes humility and brotherhood. Before entering the temple area, all men and women are required to cover their heads and walk barefoot through a small stream of water to clean their feet. These are all signs of respect, mandatory for all entering the temple space. The entrance to the temple complex itself is symbolic. There are four entrances from all directions symbolizing openness and acceptance of all. The amrit sarovar symbolizes the divine and propagates the teaching of the doctrine, to live on the earth while always keeping an eye on the divine. The domed roof plated with gold has been inspired from Islamic and Hindu architecture and is aesthetically exquisite. And while the huge influx of visitors adores the complex every day, you will find a sense of calm and serenity within the premises.

Sikhism thrives on the essence of community service and emphasises the importance of seva, as a route to negating the ego and finding peace. In keeping with the tenets of Sikhism, it is the committee that runs the place. They must be firm while assuring the discipline, however they are considerate and ever ready to help. The vibe of the Gurudwara is welcoming and hence it is a living example of community space. 'Guru ka Langar' at the Gurudwara is one of the largest kitchens in the world and it runs on the principles of egalitarianism.

Hundreds of volunteers keep the Gurudwara's kitchens running 24 hours a day. All societal barriers of religion, caste, and social status are obliterated as diners share a meal as equals, sitting on the floor in a line, known as pangat. Visiting the kitchen is an experience and you will see volunteers busy cutting, chopping, peeling and cooking the food. At one corner, there will be a group of volunteers handing out glasses of water while on the other corner sevadars will be helping the diners carry plates to the cleaning area. A team of volunteers are engaged in washing them. Some volunteers mop the floors, keeping the kitchen and the langar halls clean and ready for next round of serving.

Harmandir Sahib besides being the religious shrine also sustains the city's economy. The area around the temple has been reconstructed by the government and is now closed for vehicles. The Heritage Street or the walkway to the temple is now filled with souvenir shops and is beaming with tourists. Along the circumference of the temple area, you will find people buying toys, kirpans, papad, wadiyans, shawls and blankets. Women are busy negotiating for their Amritsari phulkari sarees and the jootis. Street vendors, small hotels, auto rickshaws are all part of the business.

The History of Building the Golden Temple
Harmandir Sahib, temple of God is the epicentre of Amritsar. The story of Amritsar is the story of the Golden Temple's foundation and survival. Sikhism was founded by Guru Nanak and taken forward by nine other gurus. The spiritual and political contestations during the Mughal era led to lots of upheavals. The gurus emphasized on their spiritual teachings and compiled it in the form of scriptures and hymns in Guru Granth Sahib. Guru Gobind Singh, the tenth and last living Guru declared that after him, Guru Granth Sahib will be revered as the living Guru for spiritual guidance. Sikhs will be guided by the holy book for all the material and

political issues of the world. Guru Granth Sahib is kept in all the gurudwaras and worshipped religiously. However, one of the oldest handwritten manuscript is kept here in Amritsar, hence it is a major pilgrimage site.

The history of building the golden temple spans across generations. The ideas of the township were forwarded by the Sikh Gurus in the past. Guru Nanak himself founded Kartarpur, it is an important place of pilgrimage. His successor, Guru Angad, chose Khadur Sahib as his central town. Guru Amar Das adopted Goindwal as the seat of his activity and constructed the holy baoli for his followers. It was his successor and son-in-Law Guru Ramdas who started the construction of the tank at the allocated site. According to the legend, when Sikh missionaries arrived in the village of Tung and Sultanwind, the proprietors of the village unhesitatingly sold a sizeable chunk of land to them. Even emperor Akbar granted a large piece of revenue-free land to the Guru's daughter. It was on this acquired piece of land that the work of the excavation of the holy tank was initiated. The place came to be associated with the idea of Amrit-sar, meaning the pool of the nectar, of immortality. Many devotees started visiting this sacred pond and few even settled down in the vicinity of the sacred sarovar. Guru Ramdas took up the initiative and invited over 50 artisan communities in the newly founded city. The artisans and the traders who came to live in this village developed new markets and the related ecosystem in the vicinity. Guru ka Bazaar is one of the oldest, still in existence in the city, and is of extremely high significance. All these developments eventually led to the establishment of the township that came to be known as Ramdaspur.

Guru Arjan Sahib, the fifth Nanak, is given the credit for the idea of the establishment of this Sikh holy land. His desire to create a central place of worship for the Sikhs led him to design the architecture of Harmandir Sahib. He proposed the idea of enlarging the tank to build the place of worship in its vicinity. Hence, the construction of the temple started in 1581.

Guru Arjan also compiled the bani of his predecessors, along with the compositions of known sants, bhagats, shaikhs and bhats. Bhai Gurdas acted as his amanuensis and wrote down every dictated word. The compilation was completed in 1604. It was installed in dharamsal, constructed in the midst of the pond, after performing all the necessary rituals. This was the Adi Granth; Baba Budha Ji was appointed as its first Granthi i.e. the reader of Guru Granth Sahib. Here, the temple got the status of Ath Sath Tirth and Sikhs from various places found a place of pilgrimage.

The Bloody Massacre In Amritsar

Jallianwala Bagh massacre, also known as the Amritsar massacre, was a critical juncture in India's national movement. It gave deep shocks to the people of Punjab as it heightened the brutality and racial subordination enforced by the British in India, and 13 April 1919 will go down as the blackest day in British colonial history. The path to independence was not an easy one and Jallianwala Bagh outrage was an attempt to crush the struggle for independence. It evoked sharp criticism both in Britain and India. Winston Churchill called it a monstrous event, an event which stands in singular and sinister isolation. The act was a shock even to those who believed in the positivity of the British rule. Undoubtedly, it was a gruesome event, unparalleled in history. The agony of India after the massacre was such that it even broke Gandhi. He wrote - "We do not want to punish Dyer. We have no desire for revenge. We want to change the system that produced Dyer". The massacre ultimately gave impetus to the anti-imperialist struggles in India and transformed Gandhi into a non co-operator. This was the beginning of the end of the British Raj in India.

On the centenary of the gruesome incidence, British Prime Minister Theresa May told the British parliament: "We deeply regret what happened and the suffering caused by the massacre."

Revisiting the Jallianwala Bagh
Walking by the narrow alleys when you reach the Bagh, you see people are hovering around the red sandstone structure that stands symbolically in the centre as a monument of remembrance. Few families are generally strolling and lounging in the green ornamental lawns while others are busy taking selfies. There is a group at the far end trying to

figure out the deathly well where so many innocents jumped to save their lives, a century back. Earlier, this bagh was a barren isolated land where cattle grazed. It was surrounded by residential houses from sides with three small exits. It was a small open place for public gathering in those days. Today, it is brimming with tourists. However, there is always some heaviness in the air that constantly remind us of the colonial brutality.

The political movements in Punjab and how it was shaping up Amritsar was a cause of concern for the British. The rising political turmoil of Punjab unnerved the colonial masters and their insecurities were depicted in the insensitivity and outrage that General Dyer demonstrated on the day of Baisakhi. Amritsar was becoming the hotbed of politics after the passing of the monstrous Rowlatt Act. Britain had won the first world war, but the global effects of the war radically transformed the fate of its empire. To control the protests in the colonies, Britishers continued with repressive wartime measures, coercive recruitment practices and the political and economic alienation experienced by the people made the Indians disillusioned.

The Britishers undertook mass recruitment of the soldiers from Punjab who went abroad to fight the British war. Back home, after the war, they were rendered jobless. While in Europe, they got exposed to the ideas of nationalism and equality. Naturally, these soldiers felt the discrimination and resented the loss of their own voices. Added to it was the agrarian crisis and apathy of the countryside. All sectors of the Indian economy faced a death blow. Hence, every Indian was against repressive British laws.

Nationalist outrage under such circumstances was obvious. To make matters worse, the colonial masters cut off all means of communication across the province and railways were uprooted. Every sense of peace was disrupted in Amritsar when a poster appeared on the clock tower next to Amritsar's fabled Golden Temple, calling on people to be prepared to 'die and kill'. All hell broke loose when Gandhi was banned from entering Punjab. In order to curb the emerging support for Gandhi's mass movement, the British government arrested and deported two local leaders from Amritsar, namely Saifuddin Kitchlew and Satyapal, both were despatched by the car to the hills of Dharamsala.

The Martial law imposed in the city was the last straw. This instigated the crowd who felt the humiliation and hence began rioting. On April 10th, a peaceful Gandhian hartal turned violent with an angry mob rampaging through the city. Its Town Hall was set on fire and government machinery came to a standstill. Telegraph and post offices were shut down after attempts of looting. This violence led to the loss of lives and property. Many Indians lost their lives and five Europeans were also assassinated by the crowd.

Following the violence, curfew was imposed in Amritsar and political meetings were banned. In defiance of the official proclamation banning such meeting, public gathered in Jallianwala Bagh. It was during this gathering of almost 20,000 people that General Dyer marched along with his soldiers and immediately after his arrival, he ordered to shoot. The British squad fired for some six to ten minutes, undertook approximately 1,650 rounds until the entire crowd fell on the ground and the few lucky ones managed to escape the death trap. No attempts were made to help the wounded and Dyer in his own words wanted to send across a message to the protestors. Even today, the surrounding walls bear the highlighted bullet holes. The victims of the onslaught were mostly Sikhs who had come from nearby villages to witness the Baisakhi fair. The worsening political turmoil in Punjab only strengthened the nationalist movement and gave the leadership to Gandhi who officially denounced any cooperation with the government and returned all the honorary medals given to him by the British government.

General Dyer's decision to open fire on the unarmed civilians led to the deaths of hundreds of Indians. The Hunter Judicial Inquiry which was constituted to inquire about the mass killings dismissed Dyer with the judgement to "retire from service on half-pay with no future prospects of employment". He proved to be an embarrassment to the British interest in India. When Dyer was giving evidences in Lahore before Hunter Committee of enquiry, he spoke of the people of Amritsar- "It would be doing a jolly lot of good and they would realise that they were not to be wicked," said Dyer about his actions at the Bagh. "I wanted to punish the naughty boy." Nevertheless, Dyer was ultimately deported from India. But before that, he became a celebratory figure among the European survivors of the Punjab turmoil. Many even hailed him as the hero of Jallianwala Bagh. The House of Lords voted in favour of Dyer during the hearing. After Dyer's dismissal from duty, a right-wing newspaper raised a fund worth 26,000 pounds for him depicting him as a victim of circumstances and a man who saved India. This gave Dyer a luxurious retirement.

It might be ironic to analyse, but the Jallianwala massacre did make the British government tolerant of public opinion and dissent. It gave the lessons of what can probably go wrong with the use of weapons to subdue to protesting subjects. The controversial Rowlatt Act, over which so much blood was spilt, was quietly repealed a few years later. The military was instructed and trained to engage with the civilians in a more mature and humanitarian way. It ensured that there were no more Dyers after 1919 and no more massacres in British India. They realised that subordination, racial subjugation and terrorism cannot help them keep their colony intact.

A Poem from Jallianwala Bagh

Few people survived the Jallianwala Bagh massacre. One such person was Nanak Singh, who was barely 22 when he witnessed the massacre. He went on to become one of Punjab's most beloved novelists. He wrote a long poem 'Khooni Vaisakhi' based on his experiences of the massacre. It is one of the most heart-warming writings on the Jallianwala Bagh massacre.

Five-thirty sharp the clock had struck
Thousands gathered in the bagh, my friends.
Voiced grievance, hardship, anger, sorrow
Saying, no one listens to us, my friends.
Those words forlorn, they barely voiced
Came soldiers thundering down, my friends.
At Dyer's command, those Gurkha troops
Gathered in a formation tight, my friends.

And fire and fire and fire they did
Some thousands of bullets were shot, my friends.

In minutes, the Bagh so strewn with corpses
None knew just who was who, my friends.
Many of them did look like Sikhs
Amid Hindus and Muslims plenty, my friends.
In the prime of their youth, our bravehearts lay
Gasping for one last breath, my friends.

Says Nanak Singh, Who knows their state
But God the One and Only, my friends.

With faces drawn and muffled sobs
They sift through the corpses in silent fear.
Like moth on a flame, hearts burn to ashes
On seeing the fate of sons so dear.
Ah! The pain of losing a child so precious

Like the heart is pierced with dagger or spear.
Grief inconsolable melts the toughest of souls
Even faces most stoic shed tear after tear.

My child, oh! Wake up just once more
What makes you sleep in a place so grey?
You left us alone for a voyage so long
No goodbye you bid, nor farewell did you say.
Couldn't you wait for a while longer
To let us join you, on your eternal way?
If Time indeed had come to part
Your parents could join, without delay.
Says Nanak Singh, You can't fight Fate
When the Master orders, you just obey.

> *[Excerpt from the long poem 'Khooni Vaisakhi'*
> *originally in Punjabi by Nanak Singh.*
> *Translated in English by his grandson Navdeep Suri.]*

Partition Of India

Cities are not just buildings and roads. It is an imagined community. Generations strive together and their culture, language, art expand over time. It is a space of belongings, a space of interaction. Cities are the places where livelihood is formed, and relationships are nurtured. This is particularly true for Amritsar and Lahore. Hailed as twin cities, they shared the common history, geography and the Punjabi ethos. Sikhs, Hindus and Muslims lived together in these two historical hubs for generations. In the past, they were important economic centres in the international trade routes. Barely, fifty kilometres away, these two cities were the locus of Punjabi culture and tradition. Lahore had been a capital city under the Mughals. Mythologically, the city is connected to Lord Ram's son Luv. Kasoor is another city in Pakistan named after Lord Ram's son Kush. The partition of 1947 transformed the lives of millions of people. It is considered to be the most devastating political transition of the twentieth century. It brought about a remarkable shift in the geopolitics of this region. The two cities lying on the periphery of the newly created border witnessed traumatic changes in their relationships. Loss of Lahore is still lamented.

New nation-states were created based on power, politics, ideology and identity. Amritsar being on the periphery, was on the receiving end of the effects of partition. Decades have passed since the vast upsurge of violence that divided the subcontinent. The profound sense of nostalgia for lost homelands and the angst of fragmented cultural identities looms over the subcontinent even today. The British came and ruled Indian subcontinent for two hundred years by

making people fight for region, religion, and identity so that nobody could stand against the British forces. Today, Indian subcontinent stands divided into three nations where it is difficult to travel. Citizens on both sides of the border make consistent abortive attempts to visit the land of their ancestors. The strict visa and immigration policy along with the constant political upheavals between the two nations have kept their dreams of visiting far from reality. Citizens on both sides of borders speak of loss and longing for undivided Punjab.

Partition and Amritsar
Partition has now defined the identity of the contemporary Indian subcontinent. Cyril Radcliffe, a British judge was assigned the grand task of drawing the borders of the two new states. The new identity of India was to be created and for this barely forty days were allotted. Remaking the politics, geography and society of South Asia was a daunting task and when the borders were finally announced two days after India's Independence what followed was the colossal wave of movement that left deep scars and trauma.

It changed the lives of the people dramatically. People lost their own sense of belonging, their homeland where they lived for generations and also brought an abrupt end to historical community life. The struggles of accommodation and rehabilitation created much resentment. Stories of survival spontaneously shaped people's attitude towards government, minorities and the concept of home. Partition brought with it the bitter experiences of loss. It was distressing to lose life, property and cultural values. Peace became a distant dream and crime against humanity was a big blow to the ethos of the subcontinent. By 1948, as the trickle of people drew to a close, more than fifteen million people had been uprooted, and between one and two million were dead in the ensuing violence.

Saadat Hasan Manto who witnessed this time wrote "The tragedy of partition was not that there were now two countries instead of one but the realization that human beings in both countries were slaves, slaves of bigotry. . . slaves of religious passions, slaves of animal instincts and barbarity".

Amritsar witnessed a splurge of violence soon after partition was announced. As the words travelled to the city that a large numbers of Hindus were being killed in Lahore and surrounding villages, the cry for retaliation went up. Both Amritsar and Lahore became flashpoints. The people were disappointed when Lahore was allotted to Pakistan by the boundary commission. Fighting took place between the city's Muslim population who were anxious for Amritsar to be incorporated into Pakistan, and the other, Sikh and Hindus, who wanted it to be the part of India. Ultimately, with the Muslims leaving the city, Amritsar lost her pool of skilled labours. Of all the cities in Punjab, Amritsar was the worst affected.

The outcome of partition created haunting effects throughout the subcontinent. The hasty dismantling of the British empire off course created the ambience of fear and uncertainty. As a result, masses retaliated in the way they deemed proper to safeguard their identities. Properties and mansions were burned and looted, women were raped to inflict community dishonour, children were killed in front of their siblings. For months, the city witnessed the mob frenzy whenever the trainloads of corpses came from west Punjab. Partition was unplanned, abrupt and the violence that followed was a temporary madness. It transformed the economic centre that Amritsar was, into a border city that was receiving influx of refugees. Most of the homeless took shelter at the Golden Temple to evade violence. There was an air of distrust, enmity, fear of life and insecurity among the people. Power went into the hands of religious extremists who capitalized the situation to establish their foothold.

India's Tryst with Destiny – Amritsar's Tragedy

August became the month that will remind us of paradoxes. Those were the times when the two countries and the communities were absolutely irreconcilable. Harrowing pictures of rehabilitation sites were rampant. Refugees streamed across the newly formed India and Pakistan border. On the other hand, India was wakening to freedom. We made a tryst with destiny. Our Prime Minister welcomed the newly found independence with the speech- 'At the stroke of the midnight hour, when the world sleeps, India will awake to life and freedom.'

Today if we look back and measure the gains and losses, we realise that our journey to independence was so saturated in blood, madness and tragedy. Amritsar's Town Hall Building hosts the Partition Museum, the world's first museum documenting the India-Pakistan divide. The preserved exhibits in the museum gives emotions to the sufferings of that period. The multiple mediums used by the museum has contributed in creating an engaging experience. To create a repository of oral histories, memories and carefully saved personal items donated by the witnesses must have been an overwhelming task. But witnessing it is equally emotional. It brings back the memories of turmoil, anguish, separation and struggles of survival. In one of the displays we see a trunk box, which was perhaps stowed with precious belongings while fleeing. At the center of the museum is a well that symbolizes the many wells across Punjab where women and children threw themselves to avoid being abducted, raped and killed by the rioters. The museum also has a space dedicated to art inspired by partition. Another corner depicts how Amritsar city was ripped apart in the violence. The museum has carefully preserved all documents such as photographs, notices, posters, newspaper clippings, Artwork from the pre-Independence era and post-partition period, all framed and put up on the walls. The museum is also trying to loop in the future prospects through one of its section 'The Gallery of Hope' where the visitors are required to write their message of peace, love and hope on a leaf shaped paper and put them up in the barbed wire tree.

Today even after seven decades after partition, the old hatred is still alive. We are back in the murk. A person brought forward in time from the murderous onslaught of 70 years ago would probably look around and will be surprised to see that the old rivalries have not faded even after decades.

A Memory of Partition

1947 Partition Archive is an online portal which has been working commendably in the domain of India-Pakistan Partition. They have preserved oral histories of partition witnesses and reading them will make anyone empathetic towards their experiences. One such story is of Balbir Singh Tucker.

Balbir Singh recalls that he used to attend a primary school near Rajawala water well in Amritsar up to the fourth grade. He attended Khalsa College where he was studying Urdu until partition when Punjabi was made mandatory. He used to play a lot of soccer and field hockey. He remembers skipping many classes to take a dip in the water well at Khalsa College. Balbir Singh shares that Muslims around his neighbourhood were mostly fruit and vegetable sellers; some also drove tongas. The Hindu and Sikh families either ran their own businesses or were engaged in day labour. He vividly remembers his two best friends who were Muslim, both of whom migrated during Partition. He never saw them leave because he was in Shimla at the time. He mentions his visit to them in Lahore in 1955 when he learned that one of them had joined the Pakistan Army and the other was running his own shop. Soon after, they visited Balbir in Amritsar as well.

Balbir Singh remembers that he was 11 years old when partition struck. Soon before the unrest broke out in Amritsar, his father decided that it would be best for the family to get away for some time. It also happened to be summer, the time when Balbir's family would often go to the hills to places like Dalhousie, Kalka, and Shimla to escape the heat of the plains. Thus, when partition stuck, Balbir was in Kalka at one of his uncle's house. When they finally got on a train back to Amritsar in mid-August 1947, it halted in Ambala for almost two hours due to rumours of an attack being planned on the train. Balbir vividly remembers this halt in Ambala, when his heart was full of fear. He remembers seeing people shutting all the windows and doors of the coaches and lying on the floor of the train in order to protect themselves in case of a gunfire attack on the train. When they returned home around August 18, 1947, Balbir's family discovered that about 20-25 people were seeking refuge in their house in Putlighar because they may have thought that it was an evacuee property. However, they left soon after. Upon returning to Putlighar, Balbir discovered that all the Muslims in the area, including his two friends, had left for Pakistan.

From the time of partition, Balbir also narrates how there was a kafila (caravan) of people that went through the main bazaar of Putlighar. Soon the kafila was attacked with a homemade bomb and the army soldiers who were escorting the kafila open fired on nearby shops and houses. Balbir was in his house and remembers being terrified that the military may come inside houses and start killing them. Soon after this incident, locals gathered and built a seven-foot high wall around the mohalla, their residential locality, for protection. He shares that locals from Putlighar were among the men who attacked a Pakistan-bound train close to the Amritsar railway station.

Another incident from the partition relates more specifically to his father and one of his friends, who both decided that it would be best to purchase one or two swords for their family's protection. They left Putlighar to go towards the inner city's Hathi Gate area to buy swords. They were able to get the swords but were not able to return home that day as the rioting and killings intensified in a matter of a few hours. Balbir Singh says that after his father went missing that day, his two elder brothers went out two days later in search of their father but couldn't find him anywhere. They then returned home. Four days after he left the house, Balbir's father returned home in an ambulance carrying dead bodies to the Khalsa College hospital close to Balbir's house. Once he arrived at the Putlighar Chowk, people known to Balbir's family safely escorted him to his house. His father told his family that he had stayed in the Golden Temple for the last four days, searching for an opportunity to return home safely and finally, a ride in this ambulance was able to facilitate that. In the aftermath of the rioting, Balbir shares that he helped out at the refugee camp in Khalsa College. He was a small child, so all he was asked to do was to serve food to the people there. In his narration of events from partition, Balbir also mentions Sarab Dhyan Bedi, the famous Indian cricketer Bishen Singh Bedi's paternal uncle. According to Balbir, Sarab Dhyan Bedi used to work for the Crime Investigation Department (CID) and helped save many lives in Amritsar.

Nineteen Sixty Five

The year 1965 has a special mention in India's modern history. It was during this time that a war broke between Indian and Pakistan, another atrocity after the partition. Earlier, Lahore and Amritsar were called twin cities, but things changed drastically after the partition. Now, it was not just about the two cities, it was about the two countries, India and Pakistan. 1965 isn't just another year for Amritsaris, it was a period that brought immense pain and struggle for them.

The war

The Indo-Pak war of 1965 was a culmination of many small battles in the region. Pakistan had tried to infiltrate the Jammu and Kashmir region to participate in the insurgency against Indian rule. This was called Operation Gibraltar. As a reaction, India launched a full-fledged military attack on west Pakistan.

Jawaharlal Nehru, India's first prime minister had died the previous year and was succeeded by Lal Bahadur Shastri. Before all this, India was involved in another war with China in the year 1962. The Sino-Indian war didn't go in favour of India and had deep impact on Indian economy and military. Pakistan wanted to make the most of this situation. The 1965 war has many international connotations; it was also seen in the context of the ongoing Cold War. This war resulted in geopolitical shift in the subcontinent. Before the war both India and Pakistan had closer relations with the United States and the United Kingdom. They depended on the western forces for their supplies. During the war, India and Pakistan felt betrayed by the western forces, and this resulted in developing closer ties with Soviet Union and China respectively.

Much of the war was fought between the two countries in the Kashmir region of India, and around several borders. The seventeen-day war resulted in many casualties on both sides. This was the largest tank battle war since World War II.

Amritsar, amidst the war
There have been many instances of battles in various areas of India and Pakistan. This resulted in international pressure to announce ceasefire on September 23, 1965.

During this war, the city of Amritsar bore the maximum brunt. More than 100 civilians died in the Chheharta area of Amritsar. The air attack from Pakistan left Amritsar and entire India in deep shock. Nobody expected that the battle between the two countries would result in the death of so many civilians.

During the air battle between the two countries, unmindful of the grave danger to their lives, Amritsaris would go on rooftops of their houses to see the fight. Amritsar witnessed the fight very closely. Initially, people were excited to see the battle up-close. It was only later that Amritsaris realized the seriousness of the matter.

Amritsar was in middle of the war now. The Indian army fought the war with bravery. It crossed the international borders and entered the territory of Pakistan. As per many reports, it is believed that Indian army captured many strategic towns of Pakistan, including Batapore, Barki and Dograi, on Amritsar-Lahore road. The army had also captured two double-decker buses plying between Lahore and Batapore. These buses were brought to Amritsar as war souvenirs, and later sent to Delhi.

Many Amritsaris would happily go to Indian occupied Pakistan territory to pick up war souvenirs. Many of the locals have some tragic stories to tell. In 2005, The Tribune published an article on the occasion of forty years of the 1965 war. It interviewed a few people who had witnessed the war in Amritsar. In this article, Jayant Sud shared his tragic memory of the war. Three members of his family had gone to Indian occupied Pakistan territory to collect few war souvenirs. Jayant's brother-in-law Rajinder Nath Verma (36), along with his brothers Maharaj Sud (23) and Raman Sud (12) wanted to collect a few souvenirs. Their servant had also gone with them. Sadly, they picked up an unexploded bomb that blew all four of them instantly. This resulted in a big loss for the family.

The UN Security Council intervened and unanimously passed a resolution on September 20, 1965 that called for a ceasefire. However, the damage had been done already.

When Patton Tanks had to retreat
This remains a favourite story of Amritsaris from the 1965 war. Pakistan had planned a pincer move to attack the holy city of Amritsar. Their strategy was to enter Amritsar from Khemkaran, using the heavily armoured and tough American Patton tanks. The idea was to isolate Amritsar. It could have helped Pakistan get an upper hand as they were losing in Jammu and Kashmir and Sialkot sectors. However, Lt-General Harbaksh Singh, under whose supervision the war was being fought, was keeping a close eye on the wireless communications of the Pakistani division commandant. He strategically made plans to fight with the Patton tanks. There are many versions of this story. It is believed that the then Army Chief General J.N Chaudhary ordered Harbaksh Singh to abandon Amritsar and set up a defence line behind the Beas river. This is what the Pakistani wanted to isolate Amritsar. Harbaksh Singh refused to follow the order, and the threat to Amritsar remained only a threat. Pakistan had to retreat the Patton tanks, and this was India's victory.

Aftermath of the war
Memories of 1965 war has its own value in the city. Though many people lost their lives, both civilians and army personnel, there were many instances of bravery which kept the city together and gave a sense of pride in the years to follow.

But no one can deny the fact that this war was something the two cities, Lahore and Amritsar, still regret. The two cities share a history of centuries.

Nineteen Eighty Four

Every year on June 6, Amritsar becomes a sight of heightened tension. This day is the anniversary of Operation Blue Star, which involved the Indian Army storming the Golden Temple. The city is filled with remembrance of the attack on the Golden Temple and its sanctity. Several marches are organised in memory of those who perished during the Army's assault. On the other hand, precautions are taken that any pre-decided protest march by some fringe Sikh organisations would not lead to violence and pro-Khalistan sloganeering. There is a call for a complete shutdown in the city on this day. Generally, policemen are deployed to keep a watch for any untoward incident and vigil the sensitive areas. The day is observed as Ghallughara Dihara, Day of Genocide. It reminds native about the devastation of the Akal Takht. The vibe in the city sends the message that the Sikh community has not forgotten the perpetrators of the attack. The pain of the attack is still fresh and the wound simmering.

Operation Bluestar can rightly be called India's political blot. Punjab was steeped into an era of militancy and this tested the secular fabric of India. Religion got enmeshed with politics in such a way that challenged the democratic ethos of the country. If we examine this era of militant violence, it was quite evident that the political demands got mixed up with the religious demands. Nobody gave primacy to ending the agitation and finding a solution to these political demands. The outcome of which was a decade long genocide in the state.

The presence of the police and paramilitary forces added to the woes of the people. The systematic killings and the human right abuses brought the government and the public into direct confrontation. The government's way of dealing with the Sikh separatists, stationed in the temple premises received a lot of flak. It was seen as a state attack on the most revered site of the Sikh community. It inflicted some serious damage to many parts of the temple complex and led to deaths of so many people who were worshippers and priests besides the separatists who were residing there. Operation Blue Star was widely criticized because it depicted the government's lack of respect for the sacred status of the shrine.

The violence and anarchy in Punjab brought about an era of polarisation and divided the people on communal lines. Taking a military action to the political problem can never be a solution. Government's decision to launch the operation on Gurupurab was equally criticized. This was the Day of Remembrance of Guru Arjan Dev and thousands of Sikh pilgrims had gathered in the Temple complex to celebrate. Launching it during this time resulted in more deaths because devotees were unable to come out due to the curfew imposed and later were killed during military operation. Operation Blue Star named after the refrigerator selling company of those days, left a gaping hole in the collective psyche of the Sikhs. It brought to the forefront the fragility of the Indian state.

Operation Blue Star and Amritsar
Amritsar has been a bustling city and religion and commerce has been its two fundamental pillars. It has developed the system of peaceful coexistence where Sikhs and Hindus have lived together with self-assurance, mutual respect and harmony. However, the gruelling battle between the army and Bhindranwale put Punjab into an abyss that grew deeper and deeper and ultimately showcased a horrific ending, the worst being the assassination of Mrs. Gandhi who ordered the operation. It was Mrs. Gandhi's last battle. Amritsar was a sullen place in June 1984. All around, there was only suspicion, rumours and fear. After the fall of the Akal Takht,

Amritsar faced many challenges. The Law and order had already collapsed in the city leading to the imposition of the President's Rule in the state. The atmosphere was tensed. Frequent army check posts kept a strict surveillance in the city. The draconian media restrictions allowed only selective information and photographs to be released. The government took control of the media and the journalists were bundled out of Punjab. Others who wished to enter were barred on the borders.

This was the battle that the Army was fighting against her own section of people. The official figures about the casualties were never believed to be precise and this led to the rumours and the feeling of suspicion. In fact, it is believed that the bodies of hundreds of victims laid in the premises for three days which was then cleared away with the help of municipal committee vans. These bodies were cremated together with no chance given to the public to claim these bodies. The state even lost credibility when they did not

disclose the damage done to the Golden Temple during the operations. On the night of June 5, the army was under strict instructions to use 'minimum force' and not to fire at the Golden Temple. But the reality at the sight compelled fierce attacks and counterattacks virtually turning the temple into a battleground. The Sikh library in the premises suffered huge losses due to the fire at the site. Valuable Sikh scriptures and manuscripts were either misplaced or destroyed. Some of them were inscribed in the Guru's writings, had historical relevance and religious importance, they were lost forever.

Amritsar which was once a cultural and religious hub had now fallen silent. Bomb blasted and dismantled multi storeyed buildings around the Golden Temple were turned into Army vigil points from where they kept an eye on any visitors to the temple. The city became a mute spectator to the massive army deployments. The army was stationed in Amritsar for indefinite period and the centre empowered them with draconian laws.

For months after the operation ended, uncertainty and helplessness loomed over the entire state. People were watched with suspicion; their vehicles were occasionally stopped at army check posts and their luggage were extensively searched. Armed police were stationed at all the pressure points in the city. They were there at the corners, going up and down the lanes, at the university premises, the Golden Temple complex and every possible place that could turn into a violent spot. The strict and controversial Arms Act led to number of arbitrary arrests. The presence of so many armed men naturally created the atmosphere of mistrust, tension, hostility and anger. It was a reign of terror that loomed over Amritsar. The losses that common businesses bore was not even given primacy. Shopkeepers, traders and businessmen lost property worth crores during the era of army control.

The Political Context

The aftermath of the Operation Bluestar wreaked havoc on the lives of the people in Amritsar. The politics of the state had begun going downhill over the years and brought the communities in conflict with one another. Amritsar being the epicentre of the movement suffered the most. The 1978 bloody clash between Sikhs and Nirankari sect in Amritsar on the occasion of Baisakhi on April 13 left 13 Sikhs dead and this was a watershed moment that subsequently pushed Punjab into the dark phase of terrorism. The main accused among the Nirankaris was acquitted on grounds of self-defence. This led the Sikh community to believe that the perpetrators of their religion went unpunished. When the leader of the Nirankaris- Baba Gurbachan Singh was killed in Delhi it was assumed that Bhindranwale had planned this assault. He was naturally considered the defacto messiah of the Sikh sentiments. Politics of divisiveness pitted communities against each other and the centre was clueless about the course of action to be taken to stabilize the situation.

Incapacity of New Delhi to deal with these sectional demands contributed to the rise of extremism in the state. Ignoring the Anandpur Sahib Resolution was a political miscalculation. Then Mrs. Gandhi suspended the democratically elected Akali government who have come to power in Punjab, with Prakash Singh Badal as the Chief Minister in 1977. Backing Bhindranrwale against the Akalis in Punjab proved to be a fatal decision for her in the years to come.

By 1982, Sikh resentment and Hindu anger were the dominant emotion in Punjab. Religious emotions were fanned by targeting the community's symbols. Instances of cow slaughter began coming into light which hurt the Hindu sentiments. Bleeding cow's heads were found in the temples. On the other hand, Sikhs faced the politics of rejection and humiliation. Those who went to attend the Asian games of 1982 in Delhi felt the subtle signs of rejection like they were frisked badly. Their experiences of harassment and subjugation naturally forced them to lean towards Bhindranwale. Basically, the state was divided. Bhindranwale had polarized the Sikhs against the Hindus to win Khalistan and Mrs. Gandhi was appeasing the Hindus to consolidate her vote bank.

Amritsar came to standstill when on 25 April, 1983 Avtar Singh Atwal was shot down in the temple premises. He was a respected senior police officer and was critical to the idea of Khalistan. His assassination in the temple premises sent shock waves throughout the state. Not only was the religious sanctity of the shrine was violated but it also catapulted Bhinderwala to a position where no one can challenge his prowess. Atwal's gunning down at the temple's entrance turned the whole politics of the state towards instability.

Added to this was the killings of the Hindu passengers in the Amritsar- Delhi bus. This event just saw the ascendancy of Bhindranwale's fear and consolidated his claim to Akal Takht which he had already transformed into an impregnable abode.

The government had to take strict actions now. It could no longer be a mute spectator to the events in Punjab. A military confrontation with Bhindranwale had now become inevitable. Amritsar was turned into a fortress and an armoured assault on one of the most sacred shrines in the country was decided upon. This decision was going to be tragic. At the end as it proved to be there were no winners, just lessons to be learnt.

The Aftermath of Operation Blue Star
The militant politics took horrific proportions with a series

of killings and retaliations. It neither ended terrorism nor religious militant politics in the state. The waves of turmoil from Amritsar reached the Prime Minister's home. There was increased threat perception to Indira Gandhi's life after the Amritsar episode and it manifested itself when she was assassination by Beant Singh and Satwant Singh on the morning of October 31, 1984. What followed her assassination brought more troubles to the Sikhs. As news filtered in that her assailants belonged to the Sikh community, a horrific anti-Sikh pogrom began on the evening of October 31.

The politics of Punjab was stepped in religion and was further entangled into Identity politics and misgovernment. The separatist campaign made the Sikhs disgruntled about their identity in the country. Democracy was challenged and nation's diversity went for a toss.

Lessons Learnt
Agreeably, India is a complex society and to keep all sections of the country contended is a difficult job. The only way out could be accommodation and compromise. The minorities need to feel wanted and develop in them a sense of belongingness. India's reality is very delicate, and a minor mishandling can alienate a community. To avoid any such catastrophe in future the government should not take recourse to repression. The roots of dissatisfaction have to be eradicated.

The Khalistan insurgency did haunt Amritsar and the Indian government till early 1990s. But what could not be destroyed was the spirit of Amritsar. Normalcy was restored after much efforts. Amritsar began reinforcing its distinctive values and ethos. It has a rich and varied history to deal with violence. The city has been torn down and rebuilt over time. But Amritsar has the capacity to spring back to its essence after every brutal strike on its soul. This ancient city has been the part of history because of many notorious violent incidents, but if you scratch beneath the surface you will find the people who are most endearing and modest. The outer facade might give a different perception, but the city and its voices are authentic. What we can celebrate is the indestructible spirit of Amritsar and the sense of solace and tranquillity with which it will embrace you.

Wagah Border and Diplomacy

The Wagah-Attari border between India and Pakistan stands as a geographic mark of the great Partition. The border is situated about twenty kilometers from the city of Amritsar and is an arena where the Border Security Force and the Pakistani Rangers daily perform the 'Retreat Ceremony'. This international check post has now become a place for celebrating the sovereignty of both nations with an impressive retreat ceremony every evening that marks the closure of gates at the international border. Any visit to Amritsar is incomplete if you have not witnessed this border ceremony.

A Tale of Two Villages
Wagah is a village in Pakistan, while Attari lies on the Indian side. These two villages bear witness to the politics of independence. Before Partition the two villages lied somewhere in between Lahore and Amritsar. The partition of India put the two villages on a higher pedestal and gave them the status of international border checkpoint between the two countries. When Sir Cyril Radcliffe drew a line in August 1947, dividing the landmass into two separate countries, Wagah and Attari, known hitherto as 'twin villages' found themselves on opposite sides of the border. The story of Wagah and Attari is a microcosm for the larger cultural links between east and west Punjab that was arbitrarily divided. It was impossible to tell one village from the other, but today the locals resent the loss caused by unnatural border division.

The two frontier villages have witnessed the politics of the subcontinent from extreme proximity. The delineation of the border between the new states of India and Pakistan in 1947 led to the creation of two nation states on the basis of religious demographics. They saw millions cross over to either side during partition. These borderline villages experienced the chills when trains arrived and departed the borders with mutilated corpses. Even today the Wagah-Attari border reminds us of that lingering feeling that partition brought to the subcontinent. The beating retreat ceremony for which Wagah is famous personifies the tension and heavy resentment that exists between both the countries and also celebrates the shared similar history and culture that represents the beautiful camaraderie India and Pakistan hold in their hearts. This ceremony is displayed with full patriotic fervour on both sides of the border, seven days a week and all the seasons.

The Arena at The Border
Borders mark identities as well as create a sense of inclusion and exclusion. It undoubtedly creates a divide of 'us' versus 'them'. This sense of national space and identity is on full display at this army outpost of Attari border. It is, moreover, the only border crossing between India and Pakistan which is operational and hence is under strict surveillance of BSF. Attari-Wagah border is no less than the checkpoint Charlie was to Berlin during the Cold War. This post can be identified amidst an elaborate complex of buildings, roads and barriers. The stands around can accommodate thousands of spectators. Every day at sunset both the countries conduct the formal state ceremony in the 'No Man's Land'. Hundreds of spectators throng the galleries built around the area to witness the ceremony. Emotions run high amongst those who have gathered here. The energy of this place is contagious. As patriotic songs are played in the loudspeakers around, the visitors begin imbibing the energy of the moment. Dancers in bright outfits enthrals the audiences and it is electrifying to see all of them dancing, hollering and radiating pride for the country. The patriotic atmosphere that is created naturally stirs up the audiences to shout pro-state slogans like

'Hindustan Zindabad', 'Jai Hind', 'Bharat Mata Ki Jai' 'Vande Mataram'. Corresponding to it one can hear slogans from the other side as well. Both sides are cautioned repeatedly not to raise inflammatory slogans to maintain the essence of the ceremony. The huge flags of the two nuclear- armed nations facing each other adds to the ambience of that abstract emotions of zeal, spirit, glory and patriotism.

The soldiers from both sides looks in many ways identical. Pakistani guards wear black uniforms; Indians, olive along with their ostentatiously colourful headgears. But all, broad shoulders and moustached, stand 6 feet 5 inches or taller, and stride about in sashes. The show at Wagah is no less than theatrics. The soldiers exhibit passion, strength and unity while participating in the ceremony. The gates on the border keeps gleaming with nation's pride as each is painted in the colour of their respective country's flag. Both the gates open up towards the end of the ceremony and soldiers from both sides march forward for that friendly crisp handshake to each other and bring the ceremony to a closure on a positive note. Towards the end, the atmosphere is filled with the sound of the bugles, followed by the flag lowering ceremony that formally brings the end to the day.

The entire economy of the area thrives on the Wagah border celebrations and can be termed as 'patriot economy'. It has evolved in this place by allowing the locals to indulge in micro businesses ranging from food stalls to selling DVD's. Commercial bazaars have sprung up near this border zone area offering specific objects like Indian tiranga, caps, wristbands, stickers of tirangas, pictures and models of BSF soldiers and Pakistani Rangers, and makeup artists drawing flags on the forehead and cheeks of the visitors.

The Border as A Tool Of Diplomacy
Wagah is the ultimate border where hostility and nationalism

is enacted every day. Although many Indians and Pakistanis share much in common, to an extent that they could be called a single entity, it is remarkable to see the stubbornness, aggression and unreason during this daily ritual at the borders. There are generally groups in the crowd, on both sides of the border, which raises slogans to belittle the 'other' country. This speaks of the reality that grips both the nations. The need for peace promotion amongst both the country cannot be avoided. An ever-increasing number of individuals, NGOs, politicians and professional groups in the two countries challenge the national security state, call for people to people contact and for peaceful resolution of all disputes. Now, that the subcontinent is a nuclear zone, the responsibility of these two global actors is also immense. Any escalation of conflict can bring disaster to the region. Wagah- Attari border witnesses the uncertainty of the political climate between the two nations that can change within a short period.

On one side there are Amritsaris who lament not visiting Pakistan to meet their relatives. They have an emotional attachment to the land that now lies beyond the borders that they could never cross. That is the land where they were born, where the ashes of their ancestors had been scattered. They demand of a visa-free regime and lifting of all restrictions on travel between both the countries. On the other hand, there are elements in the society always reinforcing negative images of Pakistan. The paradox is such that there are peace and human rights activists in both the countries including former ministers, retired military officials, retired bureaucrats, businessmen, judges, parliamentarians, teachers, scholars, media people, writers, artists and lawyers promoting for better relations and at the same time the past history compels us to think that the two countries and communities here are absolutely irreconcilable. Wagah-Attari border is the mirror of this paradox only.

As a result of the concerted efforts, the war hysteria has been subdued. Instead, there is peace euphoria everywhere. Amritsar has always been at a pivotal position when it comes to India-Pakistan diplomatic ties. In 1999 the then Indian Prime Minister Atal Bihari Vajpayee made a significant diplomatic breakthrough and travelled on a bus route from Amritsar to Lahore.

"I bring the goodwill and hope of my fellow Indians who seek abiding peace and harmony with Pakistan... I am conscious that this is a defining moment in South Asian history, and I hope we will be able to rise to the challenge." Atal Bihar Vajpayee had said on his arrival in Lahore. When he hugged his Pakistani counterpart Nawaz Sharif, it left an enduring image that symbolizes hope in bilateral ties.

Of course, we are all the by-products of our social and political surroundings. The hatred for Pakistan is historical and the outcome of the experiences of partition. Such sentiments were and still remains widespread and deeply rooted in Indian society. Perhaps what we need to understand is that lessons from history may be instructive, but one should appreciate that times change, and so do the scenarios and the futures. A series of concerted and sustained efforts will be required to make a proposal for a peace realizable among these two South Asian nations.

Part 3
Amritsari

Sudarshan Kapoor

I have lived my whole life in Amritsar. During my teenage, I used to go to Lahore to see new films. I remember watching movies like Sikandar, Pukaar, and Anmol Ghadi in Lahore. First day, first shows where amazing in Lahore. There was a shop named B. Leelaram in Lahore which is now in Delhi. People used to throng this place to get the suit of their choice stitched. There was a popular saying the region 'Lahore badshah, Ambarsar vazir, baaqi sab faqeer'.

Talks about partition started in the year 1945. We thought this will never happen. In Amritsar, Hindus and Muslims co-existed peacefully. There used to be Hindu paani and Muslim paani (different water for Hindus and Muslims) at public places. It was the solution for peaceful coexistence. I remember thandi kuyi (cold water well) near Company Bagh. During summers, the front side of the well was for the Hindus, and Muslims used the backside.

Riots started in Amritsar in early 1947. There were instances in 1946 as well but in 1947, riots took place every day. I remember, it was March 5, the first day of Holi. RSS had boycotted Holi because Muslims had killed two Hindu boys. This festival was celebrated beautifully in the city for four days. When this incident took place, the shops were closed for the whole week. I had joined RSS in the year 1940. In 1947, after this incident, I went to RSS shakha with 12 of my friends and played Holi in Durgyana Mandir. We shouted slogans against Muslims. It was fun because there was no violence. In less than two hours after the celebrations, the riots started. The whole Katra Jaimal Singh was burnt. The famous poet Manto used to live there. During that time, he was living in Bombay. Later, curfew was imposed. The whole city was on fire. Riots continued for 6 months. In the evenings, we used to count how many Hindus were dead. Life was reduced to a statistic. Most of the Muslim houses in Amritsar were burnt. The city never became what it used to be. Business never grew earlier, and city lost its soul in the tragedy that was partition.

Surinder Kochar

Amritsar is a beautiful city, truly divine. I have travelled to many places, but I am glad I belong to this city. One of the most important points I wanted to lay emphasis on is that the history of Amritsar is not limited to the city itself but embodies the important aspects of the history of Sikhism and Punjab.

As a historian and a journalist, I have invested a major part of my life in understanding the city and its culture. The city was, as we all know, founded by Guru Ram Das Ji, the fourth Sikh guru. Usually, a city is created at first and then a place of worship comes up organically, but the story is a little different for Amritsar. This city was created around a place of worship called Harmandir Sahib; it is right at the centre of the city now commonly known as the Golden Temple. Earlier, Amritsar was known by the name Ramdaspur. It is now considerably a new city with a history of less than 500 years. However, the name of the city is mentioned in many mythological stories. I hesitate to deny these claims as these are related to people's faith and I respect that.

The first residential building in Amritsar is Guru Ke Mahal; it is a Gurudwara now. There are five sarovars (ponds) in the city namely, Amritsar, Santokh Sar, Kaul Sar, Bivek Sar and Ram Sar. Later, the entire city was named Amritsar, which means nectar pond. Guru Ji created 69 Katras, colonies, in the city. These colonies were created as per people's profession and caste. Over the years, the city has witnessed various political upheavals because of its religious importance.

With each passing year, the city has registered many changes. What we see now is the modern version of the city. However, it has had its share of tragedies. I see history of the city everywhere. It would never be just another city for me. When I see a wall here, I see stories, I see decades and decades of history seeped in each one of them. I share a deep bond with the city, it never bores me rather encourages me to explore its lanes even more.

The people of the city are very helpful and cordial. It is known that the city wasn't won in a war, it wasn't created by killing anyone but had seen the light of the day due to a saint, a Guru. We walk on a pious soil; we are thus bound to help each other and be hospitable.

The food culture of the city is very exciting for me. A true Amritsari has an appetite like none other. We can eat and talk throughout the day. I had a few health issues recently due to my eating habits. My doctor has asked me to change my habits. And I asked him to give me another solution but this. Our taste buds are so enhanced that we cannot simply eat bland food. I believe, the city is bestowed with the best taste on the planet. How can we not respect such a blessing?

Vinay Mehra

Amritsar is a city of no discrimination. We have grown seeing Hindus in Gurudwaras and Sikhs in Hindu temples. Such visuals have always been a part of our upbringing. Everybody is welcomed everywhere. This is a big open home. This city has scarred memories of 1919, 1947 and 1984 – Jalianwala Bagh, partition and Operation Blue Star. Our generation does not know exactly what happened then but the those memories have been passed on to us, and we can feel the pain when these years are discussed.

I have fond memories of visiting the Golden Temple and Durgayana Temple ever since I was a kid. My grandfather used to take me to Tulsidas Temple inside the Durgayana Temple. I still visit this temple when I am around. It has memories of my grandfather and of my childhood.

I am a chartered accountant by profession, and I plan to spend my entire life in this city. I plan to travel the world but come home to Amritsar after each of those visits. This city gives me a sense of comfort in both professional and personal levels. Owing to business-oriented people in the city, I see a lot of opportunity of growth here professionally.

I and my friends like to go out for long drives in Amritsar. There is a difference between long drives and gedi. A gedi is on two-wheelers and long drives are on four-wheelers. This is our way of exploring the city and life. Gedi and long drives have one thing in common, roaming around from one place to another without any tension and destination. As per me, one of the best feelings in the world is when your friend is sitting beside you, and all you want to do is drive around, without any destination. This is how friendship grows in our city.

Amritsar is quite a vibrant city and there is never a dull moment. Food wise, this city is just awesome. I am not sure if any other city has so much food options as Amritsar.

I have witnessed many changes in the last decade in Amritsar itself. What bothers me more is the fact that greenery has reduced in the city. This is something which needs immediate attention. Amritsar is a heritage city and heritage needs care. We need to take care of our home.

RJ Heer

When I used to do theatre in during my college days, my teacher told me once, 'Waris di Heer sab nu sohni lagdi hai. Par apne ghar paida huyi Heer kisi nu sohni nahi lagdi.' Everybody likes the character of Heer written by the great Punjabi writer Waris Shah but nobody would like a Heer in their own houses. Waris Shah's story of Heer-Ranjha, the two lovers, have cultural importance in Punjab. The character of Heer was of a girl who did what she liked. People love this story but we rarely see a supporter of Heer-like character in their own homes.

People come to me and appreciate the fact that I am a radio jockey. The same people would sometimes why am I am not getting married. Everybody is concerned about a girl's marriage in Amritsar. If a girl has crossed the age of 25, then it becomes a community job to get her married. A girl has to really fight for a career of her own. This is primarily a commercial city with men taking care of business. We have very few working women in Amritsar.

I too had my share of struggle. I gave a radio audition when I was still in my college, BBK DAV College. I was in the first year and I had decided to make a career in radio. Things went well. Family members thought of it like a hobby of which soon I'll be bored. When I told them that I am looking forward to making a full-time career as a radio jockey, everybody was concerned. It was only when my parents saw me hosting a huge event with more than 2000 people as an audience, they gained some confidence in my choice of career.

Today, people listen in Amritsar and nearby cities, including Lahore in Pakistan. It is hardly 40 kilometres away from here. So yes, I do have an international audience. People from Lahore write to me regularly on my Facebook and Instagram. Recently, they celebrated my birthday in Lahore. I feel blessed to be doing what I am doing. People know me by my radio name which is RJ Heer, my real name is Geetan Kanwar.

On a side note, we are a ghee positive community. We love our desi ghee flavour. Ghee is the ultimate solution for anything in our families. I was not well for the past few days. My mother suggested that desi ghee must be applied over my neck. It will make me feel better. My grandmother suggested putting ghee in tea as well! Everybody in Amritsar has one solution to bigger life problems and that is ghee.

Sudhir Mehra

In the riots of 1947, our house was burnt. The fire of partition had touched every family in Amritsar. Our family lost everything, but it gathered courage from the ashes. We were able to survive, and the city has been gracious to our family since then.

I witnessed the proceedings of the year 1965 very closely. The war with Pakistan had escalated. We were anxious as what will happen next. Amritsar was an important part of the war then. I guess it was September 5, 1965 when we heard a loud sound, louder than anything I have heard in my entire life. We panicked. Glass door in my drawing room cracked from that loud sound. We came to know that Pakistan had attacked our city.

The very next day India attacked and took charge. It was a total blackout in Amritsar. Living in the border city can give you a very different perspective of war. I clearly remember seeing a dogfight, the fight of two fighter planes in the sky. Amritsaris used to go to the bunkers near the border areas and serve lassi to the Indian soldiers. We felt as if we were all part of the larger fight. This was our way to serve the nation.

Amritsar used to catch Pakistani radio signals as well. I remember one day the radio announced that Pakistani army had entered Amritsar and they have taken down the clock from the Clock Tower in Hall Bazaar as a war souvenir. We went to see the clock tower and the clock was still there. One thing was sure – we were not afraid. Nobody was afraid.

In later years, the period of extremism brought down the pace of development in Amritsar. After 1990s, people stopped investing in Amritsar. This was a commercial setback for the city. Once the investment went from Amritsar to Ludhiana or Delhi, there was no coming back. We have survived that period as well.

Amritsar is a pilgrimage city. People come to worship here. The younger generation is not interested in living here. Everybody wants to leave the city. They want to move to Canada, London or Australia. They do not realize that they will have to work much more in these countries. Life is better here.

I remember the old times in Amritsar, when my grandmother ensured that every family member has dinner together. We lived in a big joint family. We had a great time. That era is gone now. Though I feel Amritsar is a big family. Everybody wishes everybody. People know each other. Those are the traditional values we carry with us.

I used to play gilly-danda and kokla-chapaki when I was a child. I do not see that anymore. Children have newer games to indulge. Times have truly changed.

Chandan Prabhakar

Amritsar and Lahore are one and the same thing for us. The only difference is of the border that divides the two cities.

I grew up in Chheharta area of Amritsar. And I saw people around me laughing on the smallest of things. The city has taught me the importance of laughter in our life. People in Amritsar do not get angry on small things, instead they can make a good joke out of mundane situations. My understanding of comedy comes from the streets of Amritsar.

It is a known saying in Amritsar that at any point of time half of the city is busy in eating food, while the other half is busy in making that food. We are a food loving community.

The area I grew up in, Chheharta, is known for the famous Gurdwara Chheharta Sahib. One cannot forget the Basant Panchmi celebrations at Chheharta Sahib. It was blissful. I still have fond memories of Basant Panchmi at the Gurdwara and in my locality. On the day of Basant Panchmi it is common to fly kites. The rich people used to fly kites while I along with my friends used to collect fallen kites. And we used to fly those kites the next day. When I look back, I do not have any regrets. Rather I enjoyed every bit of the festival. The hardships of childhood have become beautiful memories in adulthood.

We never knew the word hangout. It was only when I shifted to Mumbai, I got to know about the word hangout. Our hangout was to go to a fair in a distant land with friends. We used to go out and eat as much as possible. My favourite food was the famous Amritsari kulcha. There was one Bahadur Kulcha Wala, who made amazing Kulchas. It has become slightly difficult for me to roam around the streets of Amritsar as I used to roam around sometime back. But whenever I am in Amritsar, I go to the old places where I lived. I see myself in the people of Amritsar. I see myself in the youthful mischief of young boys. I try to live Amritsar through them.

Amritsar is bestowed with the grace of the Gurus. The blessing of Gurus have made us what we are. It is also a city which witnesses all the four seasons.

Amritsar talks to you. The air, water and soil of Amritsar know you. They talk to you like no other. The reason why I love Amritsar is because you can see the sky in the city, also you can see the land as it is. This is a lesson in life. They are necessary for our growth.

Arun Kapoor

Diwali has always been a festival I waited for in Amritsar. During my childhood, I used to buy lots of crackers. I do not remember any child buying crackers worth more than 5/- and still we had enough for the whole Diwali. My grandfather would not allow my father to give me those 5/- for crackers. It was a huge amount at that time. My uncle would come from Jalandhar and ensure that I get my crackers for Diwali.

People would visit every house during Diwali with sweets. I have vivid memories of sharing sweets with my friends. Class was not a barrier. Sharing was an integral part of Diwali. It was the essence of Diwali. Now things have changed a bit. People interact mostly with people belonging to their class. The class barrier in new age Amritsar has strengthened over the decades. It is not the only change one can see. The lifestyle of Amritsaris have changed as well.

The good thing about Amritsar's culture is that everybody loves to work. My grandfather was a workaholic. And that must have been the reason why he succeeded as a businessman. He inspired many around him with his attitude towards work. People do not like to sit idle in Amritsar. They are not interested in the bank interests on their fixed deposits. It is a city which has seen many people succeed with sheer determination. People have built an empire with hard work in this city.

My grandfather, Harichand Kapoor, believed in philanthropy. He would encourage everybody to teach their children. If anybody would come to him for help regarding child's education, he would have that proverbial 100/- for the education. That time the best school in Amritsar would charge 10/- as tuition fees. He would also say that next 100/- would be given once he/she shows child's progress report. He would not ask them to show a first division or second division for the child. The only criteria was that the child must pass, and continue with education. This was his way of contributing towards a better society.

This attitude towards society inspired our entire family to serve the society. Because you grow as a society. A single individual's growth is limited to that person. But if you can help people around you grow, you are contributing in creating a better tomorrow.

Mina Chugh

I moved to Amritsar in 1985 after my marriage. I was from Bombay. Coming from a metropolis, I had my reservations towards Amritsar. It was a much smaller city in my imagination, but Amritsar has been pleasantly surprising ever since. I realized the advantages of a small city. You are never stuck in a traffic jam, unlike any big city. You know people around you. And this is a big help in a city like Amritsar.

I was one of the first few women in the city who started boutique. People were very welcoming. I was appreciated at every step. This is one thing which Amritsar gives you, confidence to move forward. In fact, many of my initial customers have their own boutiques now!

In a way, over the last thirty-four years or so I have seen a major change in the city. There was no culture of café in the city. I studied at St. Xavier's in Bombay, and there were so many cafés near our college itself. I enjoyed that café culture in Bombay and missed it here in Amritsar. Now a stroll in Ranjit Avenue will introduce you to so many cafés here. There were traditional food joints in Amritsar. But now we have so many modern food options as well. It all happened in front of me. I saw a changing face of this beautiful city. At the same time, the old-world charm of Amritsar is still intact. The walled city of Amritsar takes you back to the old times. I have not seen anything like this in any other city- it is a confluence of tradition and modernity.

But moving to Amritsar in 1985 also meant I was entering the city just after the riots. That was also the period of terrorism in Amritsar and entire Punjab. If I look back, then I see that era as a period of transition in Amritsar. On one hand city was being introduced to modernism and on the other hand terrorism was pulling back the city towards darkness.

All of us have sad memories from that era. A very close friend of our family was kidnapped by the terrorists and he never came back. We never found his body. Nobody knew what really happened with him. And this is not a story in isolation. Everybody who has survived the era of terrorism can share a story or two which will break one's heart. But we survived. We all survived the terror and triumphed it. The city has since then thrived.

There is something in the air of Amritsar which brings positivity in life. I cannot explain this. But we cannot ignore the fact that this is the city of the Gurus. They will shower their blessings on this city no matter what. Before coming to Amritsar I was not a religious person, but this city infused in me a sense of spirituality. Now, I find my comfort in Guru Granth Sahib Ji.

Bobby Badshah

Amritsar is divided into two parts, the outer and inner Amritsar. An outsider may not realise it but there is a stark difference in the way these two Amritsars function. We live in inner Amritsar which is also known by the name Walled City as it is surrounded by 12 historic walls. As the city expanded, outer Amritsar came into being.

When people talk about the vibrancy and culture of Amritsar, they are essentially talking about inner Amritsar. The inner Amritsar has been able to preserve the old-world charm of the city even today. The world-famous cuisine of Amritsar, people's food habits, the Golden temple, everything lies in the inner city.

The outer city showcases the glimpses of modernity in Amritsar. Even though many people have now been settled in the outer city, their roots remain in the inner city, which is home to the Golden Temple.

Amritsar is truly Guru Di Nagri, the city of our Guru. It isn't an exaggeration when people say no one sleeps empty stomach in the city. The Amritsaris believe that it is our duty to help others. This is what our Guru has taught us.

My two daughters are my life. They are redefining Amritsar for me. It is with their help that I am slowly understanding how modern Amritsar functions. They have their share of complaints about the city, but I think they love it too much to ever leave it.

Joginder Singh

I am not from Amritsar but now it has been almost four decades living in Amritsar. As a historian, I am very much interested in understanding the history of Amritsar. Incidentally, the history of this place where we are sitting, Lawrence Road, is very interesting. This was created by Britishers, and Indians were not allowed to live in this area. Now, this is a posh area.

My understanding of the city says that it was developed after the Jallianwala Bagh incident in 1919. After the Jallianwala Bagh massacre, Britishers were concerned for their safety. The walled city of Amritsar, what people understand as the old Amritsar, was very small and had narrow roads. Indians were all around. Britishers felt their family needed more secure area and thus the creation of new Amritsar started a century back. That is why we have Mall Road, Lawrence Road, Queen's Road in Amritsar.

Amritsar's demography changed drastically after the great partition. Before the partition many cities in Punjab had a Muslim majority population. The partition changed that. Among many losses, the partition snatched away the composite culture of Amritsar, which we miss even today. When we talk about Punjab, we talk about Sikhs, a major section of Indians think Punjabi means a Sikh person. There is no blinking at the fact that Sikhs have contributed immensely in making of what Punjab is today, but we forget the contribution of Muslims in the history of Punjab. We know Punjab in reference to a few religions but do not acknowledge many others. The scholars, including historians, have constructed hostility between Sikhs and Muslims, which was not present in reality. It is a construct of the ruling class.

In present era, sadly the heritage of Amritsar is not being preserved honestly. It is very unfortunate. A city's heritage is its history in front of the citizens. A city without heritage does not have its root. We need more honest attempts in preserving the heritage of Amritsar.

When I see the modern Amritsar, I see segmentation. We may not realize but the city is divided. A city will thrive only if we care for all.

Rajinder and Gunvant Sachdeva

Our life story is the story of everybody in Amritsar. It has been a simple life spent in a very simple city. We have lived our entire lives in joint family. Even today we live in a joint family. And it has been a blessing. The biggest happiness for us is the fact that our children live together in today's times.

Our childhood was like a dream. We used to play all the time - Gilli Danda, Kanche and so many other games. There was no pressure of studying from the family. They liked children having a good time by playing all around. We did not know each other before marriage. Now our grandchildren ask how we got married without knowing each other. How do we explain the simpler times we have witnessed in those days?

It was a time when Golden Temple used to be a place of social gathering. It was not as crowded as it is found today. People would visit the Golden Temple to catch up with friends and relatives. It was also the place where young people would see each other. Women would not roam around in the city. So, the Golden Temple was the place where love had its chance to see the light of day!

Our families met at the Golden Temple. The family members knew each other. It was a typical arranged marriage. Love marriage was unheard of at that time. Amritsaris would prefer marrying in families residing in the walled city of Amritsar itself. There were very few marriages where the bride or groom would be from outside of the walled city or from a different city. Our family members met at the Golden Temple and decided upon our marriage. We got married at a very young age, maybe at the age of eighteen or nineteen.

Films were another rage in Amritsar. Every family had one film fanatic who would see the first day first show. There was a cinema hall which would hold ladies show on Wednesday. All the women would go and see the film together. It was an event. Mothers would visit cinema hall during interval and would bring milk for all the ladies!

Amritsar is a holy city. Nobody can sleep empty stomach in this city. The city has seen dark phases as well. But the blessings of Guru Ramdass Ji have brought back its glory.

Surinder Singh

Operation Blue Star was the darkest period we witnessed. I witnessed it closely because during that time I was working as a photographer in Amritsar. On June 1st at around 8 pm, curfew was imposed in Amritsar. The situation worsened soon and there were serious consequences. Indian Army had entered the city walls. Supporters of Bhindranwale took key positions in and around the Golden Temple. Bhindranwale had earlier spoken about the possible military action against the movement. The moment we heard about the curfew being imposed on Amritsar, instead of running towards our homes we ran towards the Golden Temple. That was the common sentiment of the people of Amritsar.

Later that night, I came home. I was sleeping on my terrace and early in the morning, I woke up hearing gun shots. It was dreadful. We heard many rounds of firing. Innumerable. It felt as if the sky has illuminated with the light of firing. Our worst fear had been realised. The Golden Temple was under attack. The curfew continued for next three days. We suffered a lot; people were not able to eat as there was no way to get fresh food items. People were in constant fear as the Golden Temple was under attack. The army took control of everything. Many commoners were trapped inside the Golden Temple as the attack took place on the day of martyrdom of Guru Arjan Dev Ji. People had assembled to pray in the temple. My house was near the Golden Temple and I was trapped inside it.

On June 6, the Indian army needed a photographer since their photographer had not come. They went to a photography shop called Jeevan to look for a photographer. The owner told the Indian Army to look for me, as I had the camera. When the Indian Army came to my home, my mother thought they have come to arrest me for some reason. She panicked but they made us aware of the situation. I had only nineteen reels left in my camera. It wasn't the digital era, we had limited rolls at that time. I informed the army personnel about the same. They went with me to get the roll from Capital Studio in Hall Bazar. The owner got scared as we reached the shop, but we finally got the camera roll.

The Indian Army asked me to take the very first photographs of the Golden Temple after the attacks. The commoners had not seen the Golden Temple after the attack, and I was probably among the very first Amritsaris to see the Golden Temple in such a situation.

It was disheartening to see the Golden Temple in such condition. Akal Takht had been blown by the army tank. I could see the portions of Akal Takht in the holy pond. The army personnel had warned me to take the photographs carefully. They even threatened me of serious consequences if any of the photographs get leaked. They needed the photographs for their record purpose.

I took the photographs and was asked to develop and hand over the same to the Indian army along with the negatives. They never left me alone. I had my own setup of developing photographs at my home and they were with me all the time. I developed the photographs and hung them in my dark room for drying. Army personnel were standing outside the room. In that moment I took a photograph of the photos. I still have them.

Acknowledgement

We sincerely acknowledge the valuable inputs and support rendered by the following individuals during the course of writing this book:

Mr Amanpreet Singh Sachdeva
Mr Arun Kapoor, Former Rotary International Governor
Ms Anurit Sachdeva
Mr Ashok Sethi
Ms Avneet Sachdeva
Mr B.M Singh
Mrs Baljit Kaur
Mr Chandan Prabhakar
Mrs Dolly Sachdeva
Ms Geetan Kanwar
Mrs Gunwant Sachdeva
Mr Harpreet Singh
Mr Jasraj Singh Katari
Mr Jaspal Singh
Mr Jatinder Pal Singh
Prof. (Dr.) Joginder Singh, Administrator, Bhai Veer Singh Niwas
Mrs Mandeep Sachdeva
Mrs Mina Chugh
Mr Navdeep Singh Suri
Mrs Prabhleen Kaur
Dr Pushpinder Singh Grover, Indian Academy of Fine Arts, Amritsar
Mr Rajinder Singh Sachdeva
Mr Rohit

Mr Rohit Mehra
Mr Ronit Gupta
Mrs Shubha Guru
Ms Simrat Sachdeva
Mr Surinder Kochar, Historian
Mr Sudershan Kapoor, Advocate
Mrs Sudarshan Walia, Delia Club
Mr Sudhir Mehra, Advocate
Ms Suvreen
Mr Surinder Singh, President, Federation of Hotels and guest house Association, Amritsar
Mrs Sweety Sinha
Mr Vinay Mehra

References

These books and sources were referred to during the process of writing this book.

Punjab, Punjabis and Punjabiyat by Khushwant Singh

Amritsar Aarambh Ton by Surinder Kochar

Barah Maha (Steek) by Sikh Missionary College, Ludhiana

City HRIDAY Plan, Amritsar by Ministry of Urban Development, Govt. of India

Khooni Vaisakhi: A Poem from the Jallianwala Bagh Massacre 1919 by Nanak Singh and Navdeep Suri

Amritsar: Mrs Gandhi's Last Battle by Mark Tully and Satish Jacob

The Punjab Story by K.P.S Gill

Imagining Lahore by Khalid Haroon

India in Slow Motion by Mark Tully

1947 Partition Archive

The Tribune

Wikipedia

Google

About the authors

CA Davinder Singh

CA Davinder Singh is an Amritsar based gold medallist Chartered Accountant and a heritage enthusiast. He has been actively engaged in promoting socio-cultural activities in Amritsar. Davinder is also associated with Rotary International in the capacity of District Governor (2020-21), one of the largest NGOs in the world.

CA Davinder is a sixth generation Amritsari and was born in 1970. An alumni of Khalsa College, Amritsar, he loves to share stories of the city with the visitors.

He may be contacted at ca@davinderca.com

Nihal Parashar

Nihal is a Mumbai based content creator. He works primarily as a writer and actor for audio-visual medium. Nihal has been an active theatre practitioner for over a decade.

Born in Chhapra, Bihar, Nihal Parashar grew up in Patna. He studied at Dyal Singh College, University of Delhi, and at the Indian Institute of Mass Communication, Delhi.

He may be contacted at nihalparashar24@gmail.com

www.ingramcontent.com/pod-product-compliance
Ingram Content Group UK Ltd.
Pitfield, Milton Keynes, MK11 3LW, UK
UKHW042001230426
12048UKWH00009B/475